The Last Newspaper in the World

MICK STONE

BMS BOOKS an imprint of
Business Media Services Ltd
5 High Street
Rotorua 3010
New Zealand

Tel: 64-7-349 4107
Mob: 027-2096861
Email: ms@bms.co.nz

ISBN: 978-0-473-23249-8
ISBN-13:978-0-473-232250-4

DEDICATION

To my family

CONTENTS

ACKNOWLEDGMENTS

This story is a direct descendant of The Last Picture Show, the brilliant depiction of life in Thalia, a small town in Texas, written by Larry McMurtry. I wish to acknowledge my friend Phil who has been living the reality of changes in the media and working in a small town itself being transformed. Thanks to Felicity who talked to me about my story. Although readers may know some place names or be able to identify locations, the characters and the events in this book are most definitely fictional. A couple of verses have been used from songs: 'Nantes' written by Zach Condon of Beirut; EMI Music Publishing. 'Best Friend' by Amy Winehouse. A quote from Grahame Greene is attributed to *The Other Man, Conversations with Graham Greene*, by Marie-Francoise Allain.

1

ALBATROSS

Gordon poked the dead bird with a piece of driftwood. I stood opposite him in my wet suit leaning on my surfboard. The gull was an albatross, larger than a seagull. Finding the big bird dead on our beach was unusual and, I suppose, interesting.

'Albatrosses don't just fall out of the sky,' I said, as Gordon gave the bird a tentative prod with the twisted stick.

Gordon had been out for his morning walk before opening up his café across the road from the beach.

'Yes, and you can see how its wing is broken,' he said.

I leaned down and turned the big bird over. It tumbled awkwardly from one side to the other, its grey and white feathers dull and covered in the sand. Lying there on its back, one huge wing outstretched and the other at an L-shape, the albatross almost looked surprised at its fate.

'It's against the law to kill albatrosses, isn't it?' I asked.

'Yeah, and besides, it's bad luck.'

Gordon stood back and threw the stick into a streak of white water creeping up the beach.

'I'd better go and open up,' he said, turning to walk up to the dunes.

The broken bird came to mind again when another albatross landed near where I was sitting on my board in the surf. The onshore wind made the surf rough and difficult to ride. I liked it like that. Nobody else out, tough conditions and the occasional stand-up wave. Once I fought my way out through the grey storm surf I could turn around out the back and look in at the chaos as wave after wave crashed in no particular pattern. Patience. Don't let the thunder of energy crashing down the beach push you into taking off early and ending up in that dishwasher. So I was sitting out there alone, waiting for the wind to lessen and a set to form up into some kind of shape, when the albatross dropped into the water nearby. It was alone, most seagulls having flown inland or dotted along the white wet sand of the beach, huddled facing into the wind. Seeing that albatross could have been interpreted as some sort of omen, if I was into that sort of thing. Now looking at this big bird floating nearby, I was reminded how ugly the other bird had seemed on land and in death and yet how confident the albatross seemed sitting next to me in the storm waves. I must seem the ugly one out here and the one most at risk from a flip of the waves. The bird suddenly unleashed its wings and ran across the surface of the water before taking off. Alerted, I looked around and saw the sea changing shape as the wind had now died and waves formed into a set behind me. The first two waves passed as I paddled hard to get over them, and I could see the last waves were going to close out in a line across the bay, so I turned and grabbed the third wave. Really, there wasn't much of a face but it was enough to get up good speed before the wave broke, engulfing me as I fell flat to hang on the board for the ride in. A small flight and quite insignificant compared to the albatross.

As I stood in the shallows, with the outgoing tide pulling hard against my legs, I could see somebody waving on shore. It was starting to rain quite heavily and the torrent had forced my hair over my eyes but through the curtain of drops I could see Angelique. I looked back out to the waves and could see the surf had even in that short time reverted to mush. Down the beach, I could now see the dead albatross being pulled out from the shore by an outgoing rip. More white water was pouring in and, as I lay on my board, I saw Angelique waving again. I picked up my board and forced my legs through the outgoing stream of the tide, gave her a small wave of my hand and ran through the shallows as the rain got heavier. Even as the rain started to pepper the sand I thought how beautiful Angelique was and how I felt about her. Out of reach, of course, because she was living with a friend of my dad's, Bernard, or Bernie as we called him. A grumpy old shit as I called him. Bernie was always rarking me up and although it was hard not to like him, it was equally difficult not to be slightly jealous. All this in the few seconds it took to reach Angelique. She had already turned her back on the sea as she waited for me. She wasn't one of the current tiny beauties with long blonde hair – instead deep black hair bobbed on a cheeky round face. Round kind of described her rather than slim. She was wrapped in a raincoat, and was probably one of the few people to wear gumboots to the beach. I reached her and she turned slightly towards me, her hair dampened down and her face turned up to me, and she called out into the wind

'Bill, your father called. He's been trying to reach you urgently. Called you on your phone but...' and shrugged.

'Hi, thanks I'll get changed and give him a call. Do you reckon I can get a drink?'

'Of course, but call your father first, it sounded urgent.'

We walked up through the sandhills to the roadside and Angelique crossed over to Gordon's Seaside Store and Café. I threw my board in the back of my car, got out of my wet suit and changed in the shelter of the boot door as the rain eased. 'Urgent', everything was urgent for dad. He owned *The Coast Courier*, or as he liked to call it 'The Last Newspaper in the World'. Of course it wasn't the last newspaper in the world, although it felt like that to him as more and more local newspapers were merged into national newspapers, which themselves dissolved into media groups. Sometimes it did look like dad was the last independent newspaper owner, if not in the world at least in our niche as his contemporaries disappeared from the scene. I had tried to persuade the old man to get out of the business or at least go digital with *The Coast Courier*. Dad would pop another peppermint – he was constantly trying to give up smoking – and look at me as though there was something important I didn't understand. He'd recently added the last newspaper in the world slug line to the masthead, as if to underline his belief.

I rang dad from the café as Angelique made my coffee. The phone was answered with a 'where are you? We've got an urgent on and you're fucken missing in action.'

Swearing was second nature to dad, particularly when he was getting heated about something. He used to control it in what he called 'mixed company' and although the language used to shock parents of school friends, my friends thought it was a laugh.

'What's up Harry,' I said evenly. I had to drop the dad thing at work.

'Oh, just a small matter of a dead body found out at Waterslea. Where are you?'

'Just having a coffee and then I'll come in.'

'Nah, go straight out there and see what's happening. It's down the Drain Road.'

'Right, cheerio.'

'Now don't fuck around with this.'

I went back to my table. Angelique had delivered my long black. 'Hadn't you better get going? That sounded urgent,' she said as she sat down opposite me.

'Yeah, I guess so. I just want to stay here and flirt with you.' Her round face reddened and she frowned as she looked up at me as I stood up.

'Well, I don't think Bernie would like that would he,' she said, her eyebrows going down. I shrugged and leant over to kiss her.

'Oi,' Gordon called out from behind the bar. 'Bill Brown, leave her alone young feller, I don't want any of that carry on in here.'

Angelique laughed and gave me a quick kiss on the cheek. 'You'd better go, or we'll both be in trouble.'

Outside the rain had dropped to a light drizzle. The tide was pretty much out now and the waves looked like the ragged ends of my jeans . The road ran along the beach front. Along the same side of the street as the café, houses were mostly closed up for winter and motels had hopeful 'vacancy' signs posted. Spray from the stormy sea gave the whole place a real closed out look. I drove along the gap between the land and sea and thought about the big gull and how it ran along the waves to fly; how I felt I was flying as I dropped down into the wave. The bird flew past me, dipped then rose over the wave behind me. I turned the car away from the beach and drove over the hill to Waterslea with that sad feeling I always had when I left the beach and confronted reality.

During summer, the fields around Waterslea shimmered. Maize crops were the mainstay for farmers in the area. As the summer's heat grew more intense, the crop was transformed into fields of gold. Today, however, it was mid-winter and the fields were in stubble, a kind of lifeless grey. Waterslea had once been a swamp and although drains now ran out to the river, the area was still prone to flooding as nature once again tried to regain what it had lost.

The police had a roadblock up and I pulled over onto the edge of the road, careful not to get too close to the drain. I got out of the car, silently swearing as I saw the group of cops. The sergeant was Norm Stead. He had a face resembling a hammer and probably was at times. His muscular body could be taken for that of a body builder but it was all natural – he'd always been a big prick. Standing next to him was Jimmy Tatua. I'd been at school with Jimmy and we gave each other the nod.

'Took your time,' Stead said. He had a surprisingly high voice for such a big man.

'Well Norm I knew you'd have it all under control,' I replied. Stead didn't bite, which was unusual, and just muttered 'Sergeant Stead to you arsehole.'

'Bill, you need us more than we need you right now,' Jimmy said.

We backed off and Stead gave me a look, with a kind of smile that even now I wonder if I should have paid more attention to at the time. Remembering Harry's urging, I got down to business.

'So Mr Stead, what's happening? You've got a body, right?'

2

THE BODY IN THE DRAIN

Stead looked agitated, as if he was going to get into one of his rants but then said: 'Got a camera?'

'Yeah, but it's at the office.'

'Good, it's not much use there, follow me.' He walked down the road and I stood there for a moment, stunned.

'What's he up to?' I asked Jimmy, who shrugged.

'He's the boss here, you better go. I have to stay here and man the roadblock.'

'I'll come around to your place later.'

'Yeah, be careful with Stead. I don't know what he's up to.'

I quickly walked after Stead who was now making his way down a track off the road on to a flood bank dividing a low-lying paddock and an outlet stream. He waited for me as I leapt over the wire fence on to the bank beside him. As I stood up straight I realised we were about the same height, except I was weedier.

'Before we go any further, I'm only doing this because I owe your dad one,' he said, giving me a hard look.

'One what?'

'One whatever, come on.'

What did Stead owe dad? I filed this for discussion with the old man, but only if I could get really interested.

We walked along a narrow track on the bank. It was damp and I was suddenly feeling the cold. Not long ago, I had been sitting on my board in the middle of a winter storm and only felt cool but warm. Now, here, walking down the track behind Stead, I felt chill. As we came to the end of the drain, I could see a blue tarp half in the drain and half up the bank. We stopped and looked down the bank. I looked at my watch. It was 9.30 a.m. but it didn't matter, it was only a nervous reaction, because I knew Harry would be 'holding the front page' as he liked to say in his hushed, dramatic tone.

'Okay Stead, what's the story?'

'Wait there,' he said.

Scrambling down the bank, he gently lifted up a corner of the tarp. Lying on his back, head half submerged in the drain was Barry Brand, the mayor of our little town. He had a neat hole right in the centre of his forehead. His arms were spread in an L formation not unlike the big, dead bird. Stead had his back to me as I got my phone out of my jacket pocket and shot off a picture with the camera. Stead heard the click and lunged back up the bank.

'Give me that.'

'Too late, Stead, I've sent it already.'

He got up really close to my face, almost nose-to-nose.

'Well, tell Harry if he uses that, you'll be banned.'

'Sure, but I'll say you approved and actually led me here.'

Stead said nothing, but jerked his head towards the road and we walked back along the flood bank. I was suddenly feeling warm.

Jimmy was still at the barrier where a couple of other cars with the logos of city media outlets were parked.

'Jesus, this is going to be a bloody circus,' I heard Stead say behind me. He grabbed my shoulder and said quietly, 'Just go straight through, in your car and get out of here. And remember, no photo or else.'

I shrugged his heavy hand off my shoulder. I told Jimmy 'catch ya later' and he gave a nervous look behind me. Media teams were getting out of cars now and starting to shoot questions to Stead. Luckily, as it turned out, I'd come straight from my morning session in my own car. With jeans and jacket, and salt mangled hair and board in the back of the wagon, I was just some dude who happened to be out at the scene. I gunned the car down Drain Road and felt alive. Before heading out into the highway back to town, I pulled into the gravel on the side of the road and sent the pic to dad, saying 'Harry, check this out.' Okay, I hadn't sent it back at the drain but how'd you know, right?

Driving back into town I saw how the clouds had started clearing and tried to think about how a change in the wind would clean up the waves. Might even be good for a few waves later that day, I thought, but dad will probably go nuts with this story. So maybe tomorrow morning would be soon enough. I kept on thinking about the surf and by the time I had reached our office the story had written itself. Although I didn't really have any passion for the news business - I really just hung around town for the surf - I did have that lucky knack of being able to write stories without really expending too much effort. This infuriated dad, of course, his first love being the 'word' and all that. At least once a week we had one of those 'get a life' moments, where we reached a stalemate in an argument over a story. Usually he'd just end up shrugging his shoulders, telling me to 'well, fuck off and do some filing or whatever.'

The newsroom offices were upstairs. Downstairs were the advertising and subscription services and out the back was the printing hall. The narrow wooden stairs went straight up, so when I was a little kid I had the sensation of climbing up into another world. When I reached the top, I went over to see Glen, the chief reporter. He'd been around the paper as long as dad, but they were an unusual team – Glen being as quiet and amusing as dad was vocal and abrupt.

'Hello wanderer, how's the surf?' Glen asked. He should've been stressed out because we were already running over deadline but he seemed remarkably calm.

'Crap really, but it's good to get out. I saw...'

'So what've you got for me? There's a small hole on the front page awaiting your offering.'

'Yeah, I've got some stuff from out Drain Road. How's Harry?'

Glen looked over to the office where dad was staring intently into the computer he always seemed to have an uneasy relationship with.

'Okay. Check with Diana what she's got from the cops and let's get this paper out quickly.'

I walked over to my desk and was just about set to write when I heard the sound of a chair crashing from dad's office.

'Jesus fucken Christ.' Harry stood in the doorway of his office. He wasn't quite as tall as me, and was squarer with his tightly cut grey hair matching his close cropped beard. He was now looking intently at me, as the room went quiet.

'What is this you've sent me? You'd better come in here. You too Glen'

Glen shook his head as I passed his desk on the way into the office.

'Sorry Harry, I thought you'd have seen the pic already,' I said as we went around dad's desk and looked at the screen. Actually, the picture hadn't come up too bad and was quite sharp given it was shot off in haste from a phone. I heard Glen give an intake of breath.

'So you're telling me we are looking at a picture of this town's mayor with a bullet hole through the middle of his head? When were you going to favour us with this unimportant slice of news? Glen, did he tell you?'

Glen was blinking rather rapidly. 'Well, yeah, he said he had something for us.'

'Bullshit.' Dad didn't buy that.

'Not a bad pic isn't it,' I said hopefully.

'So who was out there?' he asked.

'Stead. He took me down the drain there.'

'Why'd he do that? It's totally out of the ordinary.'

'Harry, he said he owed you one. Didn't say what though.'

'Sure, he owes me. Did he let you take the pic?'

'He wasn't too happy about it.'

'I bet he wasn't. Glen what do you think? Should we use it?'

'Well, there's a small matter of good taste isn't there. And did he say we could use it?'

Glen and Harry looked straight at me. I don't know why, maybe just because I suddenly could still feel Stead's hard face right in mine, I said he hadn't said we could use the pic but, then again, he hadn't exactly said we couldn't. Dad closed his eyes for a moment then said: 'Okay, let's use it Glen. Just block out the eyes and the top of his head. Get going and let's see some copy.'

Before going back to my desk, I went over to see Diana and checked out what she had. I should point out here, right now, that Diana was favoured by dad. And he didn't have favourites. He never swore at her and only ever discussed her in a quiet manner. She was a university graduate with an inquiring mind. What was not to like for dad, I suppose. It did raise the question of why Diana was here working on Harry's 'last newspaper in the world'. She was the daughter of an old friend from 'back in the day', as dad continually recounted. Her desk was orderly, almost too much so. She was very good at working the phones and researching stories online. 'Just leave her alone and let her do what she's good at,' dad would say to me when I mentioned Diana didn't get out a lot. Like I said, he seemed to favour her, as he was always too willing to kick me out of the office, even if it was just for a local dog show. Technically, although I had been rubbing along with Harry in the business since I was kicked out of my last school and had more experience, Diana was the better journalist. Not that I'd ever say that out loud but she did have a real interest in the whole process. If I was texting my mates to see if the surf was running, she'd be online checking out the news of the world. As she alternated between her screen and note book, the blonde hair swung backwards and forwards. I looked over the shoulder of her paisley sweater to see what she was doing.

'Bill, I'm just finishing this up. If you have anything you want to add from the scene, you'd better enter it now.'

'Yeah, I've got something.'

'What, a description of the drain?' I gave her a quick look but she was concentrating on her screen and there was no sense of sarcasm, just a statement of fact. I read what she had so far:

```
    Police are investigating the death of a man
after a body was found near Drain Road this
morning.
```
The opening line said.

```
    The body was found by farmer Elliott Hape in
a drain when he was on his way to clear what
he thought was an obstruction to the outlet.
```

And so on. All good facts.

'So why don't you change that?'

'Ok, to what? What'd you pick up out at the drain?'

'Do you mind,' I said and reached over to her key board. 'How about this?'

```
    Mayor found slumped in drain shot between
the eyes.
```

Diana's head jerked back and she looked around at me.

'What are you saying? You've seen this? When were you going to tell me?'

I shrugged. 'Well, at least this combines both our stories. I didn't know he was found in the drain. When I saw him he was on his back beside the drain with his brains blown out.'

Diana's face had changed from one of efficient order to actual concern and she reached out a hand to lay it on my left arm, asking me how I was coping. Soft like. I shrugged, again, and said I was fine, which I was really, even though it's not every day you see somebody you know with a hole in their forehead. I don't know why I wasn't more upset actually, or 'shocked and appalled' as Glen was apt to drop into the opening pars of stories for us. I just thought how beautiful Diana looked at that moment, before she turned back to her screen.

I went back to my desk and reeled off the relevant facts. Glen pulled our words together to merge our varying stories. Harry and he agonised over the final result for a few minutes but the office door was closed, so I couldn't quite hear what they were saying. Anyway, time was against them and eventually Harry pressed the button so it was gone. The murder was biggish news that night, although not quite leading the news and not quite making the top story for the big stuff news web sites. A body found in a drain wasn't totally big news when murder was an everyday event. Of course, nobody else had the facts we had. Even I was puzzled as to why Stead should do what he did. I wondered what he 'owed' dad for that was so big he'd break with the normal practice of shielding a victim's identity.

I found out the next morning. The wind had dropped away to the south and I was on my way to the beach, so I could just about see the clean lines of surf in my mind as I drove over the hill. My phone went. It was Harry.

'Your friend Stead has dropped us in it.'

'What do you mean?'

'I've just had that prick Fish Marren on the phone saying we're banned and will get no further information or help from the police on this story.'

'What? Why?'

'He reckons Stead didn't show you the body and he certainly didn't clear you to take that pic.'

'That's bullshit,' I protested but added, 'he certainly took me to the body and lifted the tarp.'

'And the pic? Did he let you take that?'

'Well, he knew I'd take it.'

'Come in now and we'll see what we can do.'

Back at the office, it was all very quiet. Diana was staring intently at her screen as I walked by her desk.

'You're in early,' was all Glen said, without looking up at me. I automatically closed the door when I went into dad's office. Harry was chewing hard and one hand was hovering over a bag of peppermints ripped open on his desk. He looked at me with the disappointment parents reserve for their kids.

'Ok, we know this is bullshit but the photo was dodgy wasn't it?' He looked at me and waited for an answer. I just nodded.

'And?'

'I'm sorry. I just messed it up. It's just that that Stead's such an idiot. I couldn't help myself. Besides, he owed you one, didn't he?'

'Yeah. He owed me one alright. I just hated giving old Fish an opportunity to shove one up me.'

Steve 'Fish' Marren was the local police commander and dad had run a number of columns snidely comparing rising crime rates locally to the time in lieu days Fish spent out chasing yellow-fin tuna. It didn't help when Harry ran the headline 'Coastlands Police – we never catch our man' after one criminal case was chucked out of court.

'Come over here.' Harry got up and went over to one of the arm chairs to the side of his office, motioning me to sit in the other. 'Ok, I'm going to tell you something now and I don't want you to repeat this.'

'Sure, sure,' I said.

'Bill, I'm not mucking around now. Are you listening? Do you know what I mean?'

I nodded.

Now, I suppose I can tell you as I feel I can trust your judgement. What dad told me was this: As I've already said, Diana came to work for Harry because he was an old friend of her father, Bob Macdonald, who was now a high-level political lobbyist. So he trusted Harry to take his daughter under his wing on her first flight out of university life. Macdonald also knew Stead back in the day, so it was natural that he should invite Diana for a drink at the bar where the local cops regularly hung out after their shifts. Dad wasn't that keen, as the place was a bit sleazy, but Stead was an old friend of Macdonald's, so he dropped her off at the bar after work.

At about 10 that night, the phone went. It was Diana, she was sobbing. I was in my room looking at a movie on my lap top. I heard the door slam and Harry's car leave but didn't think anything of it. He was quiet when he came back and didn't say anything. Now he told me he had found Diana in a distressed state. After a few drinks, Stead had taken her back to her motel room and invited himself in for a cup of coffee. Harry didn't go into details, but it seemed to me basically Stead had raped her.

"Really?" I said, and involuntarily looked over my shoulder at Diana.

'Technically, I suppose it might be attempted rape but..." Harry said.

"So what'd you do; why is he still walking around in police uniform?" I asked.

Harry shifted in his chair and looked over my shoulder towards Diana.

"I asked her what she wanted to do but she was too confused and didn't want me to tell anyone, particularly not her dad. I wanted her to lay a complaint but she didn't want me to because Stead was a family friend and it would destroy everyone concerned.'

'So what did you do?' I asked.

'I went to see Stead the next day. He's such a cold bastard. He just said that she'd given him the go signal and maybe they'd both got mixed messages. Didn't seem to see the fact that Diana was his old pal's daughter as a real problem at all. I threatened to take it to his boss but he argued that that'd destroy not only him and his family but also Diana and her family. I guess I was persuaded, fuck it. He said he owed me.'

'So him allowing me to sight the mayor was payback, or payoff.'

'Looks like it but I'm guessing it was meant to be without a pic of Mr Brand actually lying there dead.'

3

EEL AND EGGS

The TV networks and national news were well into the story and we were shut out. We were all meant to be excited about our status as the banned media and devising new ways to cover the story. But it really was dead ends all around. Not that I minded too much. A bit of a show of calling around a few contacts for some platitudes about Mayor Brand contributed to a spread about his life and times. Diana was on to it, checking out his Facebook page for unusual pics and notes of interest but Brand just didn't seem to be that guy. It was all pretty pallid stuff, frustrating if you were looking for colour to use in a story short on detail. A not bad looking surf was just appearing on screen from the web cam when I noticed dad gesturing for me to come into the office.

It's funny how slowly a computer screen can close down when you're anxious about something. Not that I was too worried. After all, this was now a story officially going nowhere, at least as far The Last Newspaper in the World was concerned. Not so, according to Harry. He was chewing down hard on his peppermints.

'How's that mate of yours, Jimmy Tatua?' he asked, fiddling with a pen over a pad. I had a funny feeling I was being interviewed for a job, or maybe the old man having another crack at writing his memoirs.

'He's okay. I saw him the other day out at Drain Road.'

'Yeah, I know that. What does he make of this mess with your pal Stead? What does he reckon is the story about Brand?'

'I don't know, I thought we weren't allowed to talk to the cops?'

'Bullshit. I'm not going to be told what we can and can't fucken do by that bastard Stead or his useless boss.'

'But how can we? If I contact Jimmy, mightn't he get into trouble too?' Ok, I felt pretty lame but I wasn't really that interested in getting tied up in one of Harry's dramas. I'd seen too many of them over the years.

'Listen, Bill you're the reason we're in this fucken mess. If you hadn't have been sucked in by Stead, we'd still be in the game. So it's your mess, I want you to start cleaning it up.'

'But dad, surely it's your...' He cut me off at that and went over to the door and called in Glen, Diana and Neil Rabistock. Neil was the office kid, straight out of school. Harry was probably the only editor who still hired raw kids with graduates being so cheap. Neil was slim, lanky with what looked like an amused expression on his face. He seemed to spend a lot of time doodling or watching YouTube clips. Then I would read really well researched and polished stories and wondered how he did that? Looking over his shoulder one day, I saw he was drawing cartoons. Mine wasn't that flattering as I seemed to be half asleep, although it was probably a post-surf chill. Now he trundled in behind Glen and Diane and I realised then how alert his eyes were, taking everything in.

'Ok, I'm sick of us sitting on our hands. Anybody got any ideas?' Harry asked.

Before anybody could say anything, I said: 'Look, why do we have to do what the cops want?'

Why did I say that? It came out of nowhere. Well, not entirely. While Harry had been going on his rant about Jimmy and my role in the mess, I had been half listening but had somewhere else also been thinking of alternatives. Harry and Glen looked at each other. I could feel myself suddenly wound into their world.

'Yeah, go on,' Harry said.

'Well, you and I know just about everyone around here dad,' I said pointedly using the familiar. 'Somebody must know something, yet nobody seems to asking them the right questions.'

Harry looked at Glen and they exchanged a look. Although I hated dad's swearing, I couldn't help quietly giving myself a 'fuck it'.

'What's that,' Harry said.

'Nothing, what do you think?'

Glen was in deep thought. I could tell that because he first ran a hand through his greying goatee and then ran it over his head as though running through his wisps of hair.

'Yeah, I reckon we could do it, Harry. Bill can get out there and start talking to everyone you guys know, or don't know. Diana can get on the phone and call everyone else.'

Diana opened her mouth to protest, but Harry put his hand up. Glen nodded toward Neil.

'Neil, I think, can go down to the council and get all the agendas for the past year.'

'I can download them.'

Glen shrugged.

'Well do it but get a hard copy of the latest one also.'

We started filing out of the office when Harry called me back. 'Bill, are you okay with this?'

'Sure, why?'

'Well, this could get pretty heavy going, so I was wondering.'

'You don't think I'm up to it right?'

'Come on. I know you'd probably prefer to be down the beach, or anywhere but here. This is important. If you've got any problems, talk to me. Don't just drift off on me.'

'Don't go all fatherly on me all of a sudden.'

'Well you're here aren't you? Ok, bugger off and do some work.'

So ended the father-son chat. I left Harry's office, and returned to my desk, where I picked up my bag. Diana was still annoyed at getting the desk job but we swapped phone numbers in case we needed to be in contact. Leaving the newsroom, I stopped for a moment at the top of the stairs. Looking down, I could see brief sunlight flooding in through the door and I momentarily had the sense that my life was going to change. I felt a sensation as though I was stepping off into the new, even though I knew I had been there before. As I started down into the pool of light, the door at the bottom of the steps was flung open. A figure shimmered in the glare and then became Christine Dobson, another of dad's youngsters, who acted as sports and racing correspondent. Compared to Diana, she was casually dressed, jeans, sweater, ponytail over hoody jacket, and boots, muddy. Having a bit of an interest in horses and the risk of gambling, I'd had a few brief conversations with Christine but that was about all. So we nodded hello to each other. Just as I reached the door she called down to me from where she was standing now near the top of the stairs.

'Hey, Bill are you doing this thing with the mayor?'

'You mean the mayor's murder.'

'Yeah, yeah, yeah. I thought you might be interested in something.' I walked back up the stairs to her, wondering what Christine could tell me.

'It's just that when I was out at the track trials the other morning I saw Mr Brand.'

'Bit of a horse fancier was he?'

'That's the funny thing really. I'd never seem him at the track before, well, at early morning training anyway.'

Now that was possibly interesting, I thought, and turned to go.

'Oh, and he wasn't alone.' I had an inkling of why Harry swore so much. Maybe I was better off going for a surf.

'Who was he with?'

'I don't know. They were on the other side of the track but I could see them through my glasses. The other guy was in a suit. I didn't recognise him from around here. He looked like a real city type.' I wondered what that was like.

'Ok thanks.' I turned to go and then it was my turn to call out to her. 'Hey, Christine, any chance you can let me know if you come across anything more?'

The sunlight had disappeared when I turned to go out the door and it was starting to rain again. It was that light but piercing rain which was in some ways worse than a hot and heavy downpour. Standing in the doorway, I sent a message to Jimmy to say I was going out to his place and he came back with an 'ok'. Jimmy lived at home in Victory. I always got on well with Mr Tatua, maybe formed through our relationship with the sea. The Tatua family had a boat building business on a piece of land on the outskirts of Victory, even though it was 20 minutes' drive inland from Coastlands. He specialised in designing and building the kind of boats used by community groups, search and rescue and customers wanting no fuss vessels.

Although I hadn't seen him for a couple of years, we greeted each other and he welcomed me up the back steps of his house.

'I'm just going to have some kai. Do you want some?' He was slicing eel and laying the pieces out in a frying pan.

'Sure, please, that'd be good.'

Standing beside him as he cut some more chunks off for me and chucked them into the bubbling oil, I looked out the kitchen window to the back of the property. Over the wire fence at the back of the section, and across the farmland beyond, I could see the distant ranges swimming in low clouds and rain. Rows of eels hung in a lean-to at the rear of the section. It was possible to stand there with sound of frying and the occasional rumble as trucks went down the highway, to feel the stillness that belongs when you connect the dots in a life: the bush, the eels, the frying pan. Mr Tatua had also fried a couple of eggs each for us and he got me to butter some thin-sliced white bread. He said grace and we were eating at the small kitchen table when Jimmy came in, giving me a nod and jerking his head towards the back door. As we went out, Mr Tatua called out that he'd make some tea and I said that sounded good but Jimmy ignored him.

'You know we shouldn't be talking,' Jimmy said as we stood on the back porch.

'So what are they going to do? Bust one of their own?'

Jimmy looked sceptical.

'Stead is pretty hostile to you, so just be careful is all I'm saying.'

Jimmy was taller than me and dressed in his uniform stood impressively next to me on the back steps. He wasn't bull thick like Stead but looked powerful.

'I know what you mean but it's just that Harry's pushing me to get an in on this story. Have you got anything?'

'Look, I'm not going to tell you anything about what we have or haven't got. What I can say is that there's something iffy about the whole thing.'

'So it's not just a case of the star-crossed lovers.'

'I'm not saying. Could be. I don't know but I am hearing nothing on that angle.'

That was it.

He told me to leave then and as I turned to go I asked him 'Jimmy, do you know anything about the race course?'

'No, except we used to lose our pocket money there. Such a dump but a lot of money's gone down the drain there.' For a boy from Victory, Jimmy really was turning into a puritan. 'Hey what say we grab some waves soon?'

He laughed at that and shut the door.

4

TWENTY CENTS AND HORSE NINE

Instead of heading back into town, I turned left and went across the bridge into Victory. In summer there were usually kids on the bridge, jumping into the river to cool off. Often during summer a cop was parked in the main street to pick up holidaymakers passing through at speed. Victory, instead of being a place of triumph, was the kind of place you really wanted to drive through fast if you were a family of holidaymakers, returning sun burnt and a little reluctantly from the beach. This reverse reality was one reason why I enjoyed visiting Mr Tatua. The reality of people's lives in such places is so often different to those imagined by passers-by. Turning right, I went out to the race track, passing a row of tall pine trees acting as a wind break on the plains. The race track was quiet and, as I got out of the car and walked over to the rails, a light rain was falling and the wind was struggling through the pines. Across the other side of the track I could see a horse and rider cantering along in a training gallop. Nothing about the track gave any immediate impression of something worth dying for, a bit of turf in the middle of a bit of a hard case district. Maybe the mayor's meeting with the well-dressed visitor on the far side of the track the day before his death was just a coincidence.

As the rain eased and a weak sun tried to break through, the horse and rider ran into the home straight, picking up speed. The horse looked to be a young brown gelding with a tawny mane and tail. Pretty plain really but moving very well even on the sticky winter surface. I recognised the rider as Pat McComb, or '20 cents' as most people knew him. Why he was called '20 cents' was never really clear. Maybe it had something to do with his stock reply when punters asked him if a horse was worth backing that it was worth putting 20 cents on. Although I'd liked horses when I was a kid, gambling wasn't my thing, but it had in the past been Harry's. Pat and Harry had been friends for a few years but didn't see so much of each other now as Harry became obsessed with The Last Newspaper in the World. Pat cantered past on the young horse and slowed it down to a walk before turning around at the end of the straight and trotting back towards me.

'Hiya 20,' I gave him a wave as they came back down the track towards where I was standing near the finish line. Some sun was shining through, although the wind seemed stronger.

'Bill, hi, what're you doing here?' Pat called as he jumped out of the saddle and hit the turf lightly. A former taxi driver, he ran some horses on a property near the race track, mostly training up fillies and colts for trials and early races. Pat was in his late sixties but had that happy knack of looking younger. He walked over to the rail, short but not pinched thin like a jockey.

'How's your grandfather?' he asked. Some surprise must have registered on my face, because his smile momentarily dropped and he looked confused. I had forgotten that Harry wasn't really my dad, even though I called him that. Harry had brought me up since I was about nine and my parents had been out of the picture since then. When I was a kid, it just seemed right for me to call him dad. When you're in your early twenties, things do start to get a bit more complicated.

'Harry's fine. I'm just out and about trying to figure out why our good mayor ended up in a ditch with a hole in his head.'

'Yeah, I saw you cocked that story up. The cops have banned you, right? That'd make Harry even more delighted than usual.'

'Nah, he's surprisingly okay. We're just trying to work around it.'

Pat nodded and stroked the young horse's nose.

'Not much to look at but he's getting stronger,' he said, holding the reins at arm's length looking appraisingly at his charge as the horse shook its head.

He looked set to go, so I asked 'Hey 20, somebody was saying the mayor was out here the other day. Any idea as to why that might be?'

'Not for the view,' Pat said as he pulled the collar of his jacket up and gave an involuntary shiver. He and the horse were starting to cool down quickly after their run.

'He wasn't alone. He was with some suit. Is there anything going on out here of interest do you think?'

'Well, the only thing I know is that the racing club is just about on its last legs financially. But isn't that old news? A few guys have been cooking up schemes, but they're dreamers.'

'What've they been dreaming about, these guys?'

'The usual stuff; selling a bit of this, doing a bit of that, you know. Anyway, I better go and give this horse a brush down before we both get a chill. Say hi to Harry. I'll let you know if I hear anything.'

As he walked the horse away down the track I called out after him: 'Hey got a tip for Saturday?'

'Yeah put 20 cents on number nine in the third.'

I could see the old guy walking up the concourse to the horse boxes in my rear mirror as I drove away. I made a diversion to the beach. Winding down through the bush, I could see the tide was way out and narrow lines of waves walked through rips. Later, with a high tide, and a change to an offshore wind, I'd expect the surf to stand up nicely. Maybe, but my mind was elsewhere as I pulled into the car park outside Gordon's, tyres crunching on the wet sand and shell mix. It really was winter, just me and two seniors I only knew as Mr McKenzie and Mr David. Mr McKenzie, who had retired to the beach from a large farm inland, was smartly dressed with a tie and a driving cap and Mr David, who seemed to have been at the beach forever, was shabby in a coat with wet hair plastered across his forehead. Quite different, they seemed always to hang out and grumble quietly to each other. Today, they seemed to be having a laugh at something as I came through the door. It felt unusual.

Angelique was alone and greeted me with a smile as I ordered my long black. God I loved her round smiling face and strong lips. Sitting at a table near the front, I could look out over the road and just see the tops of the surf in the distance at the end of grey wet sand. I didn't think about our dead mayor, the newspaper or my role in the story. Instead, I was thinking about what old Pat had said about my grandfather. Moments like that had long since failed to bring me up short, yet just occasionally I was caught unawares. Harry was and always would be my grandfather. He had looked after me for so long I had effectively shut out memories of my parents. They only existed in another world, one where the commune was more important than the family and I learned to roll joints at an early age. Harry had bought The Last Newspaper in the World down the coast at about that time and had rescued me. It must have been dramatic at the time but I could only remember driving down the coast in his old car, between cliffs covered in flaming trees and the empty sea. So, even though he was terse and swore every second sentence, Harry became my dad and legal guardian.

'Bill, are you okay?' It was Angelique. She put my cup of coffee on the table, alongside some hot water, and sat next to me holding my hand as we looked out the window. The old guys left and walked off in opposite directions in the light wind. Angelique stood up and went over to lock the door and turn the 'Closed – back in five' sign to face outwards. I went over and wrapped my arms around her waist and kissed her neck behind her right ear. 'Not here,' she said as she pushed me back. As we walked hand-in-hand out to the back room, I could feel my history fall away bit by tiny bit. Radio Zd was playing a song by Beirut:

'It's been a long time, long time now
since I've seen you smile
and I'll gamble away my fright
and I'll gamble away my time
and in a year, a year or so
this will slip into the sea

nobody raise their voices
just another night to mourn to
nobody raise their voices
just another night to mourn to'

'Too mournful,' Angelique said as she closed the door and shut out the sounds. For a moment there was only her and me and four walls of the room stacked with cartons of tea, canned food and dry goods. I looked down at her and we kissed. And, as we kissed, the sadness left me and was replaced by a spirit of opJimmystic love. We embraced. I must have squeezed too tightly, because she pushed me back slightly. A fumbling attempt at the front of her smock was stopped by her nimble but firm fingers. 'Not now, just hold me,' she said quietly. We were like that for a few moments. Then I could feel the life going out of me and my reality draining back in. Gordon's van was pulling up outside as we went back into the café. My coffee was cold but I heaped it with sugar and downed the sweetness.

5

HELPFUL GEORGE

Gordon came in through the back of the store and brought a pile of national dailies into the café. He threw one of the fat city daily papers on to the counter.

'These city papers don't get any smaller,' he said, adding 'it looks like your murder has been bumped off the front page already.'

I stood up and went over to the counter, opening up the paper to find the story featuring on page 4 of The Herald under a 'mystery surrounds' headline.

Gordon was stacking supplies for the café and asked me what I thought.

'Yeah, it's a real mystery,' was all I could offer.

'Still, big news for you guys, I suppose,' Gordon said.

'Yeah, hey, do you know if the mayor had any interesting business connections?'

'Nah, he's out of my league,' Gordon said.

Turning to the racing page, I looked at the runners listed for Saturday's races and suddenly smiled and laughed.

Angelique, who had been clearing the dishes, looked up at me.

'I see you are happy now.'

'Yeah, an old bloke gave me a tip this morning for the races on Saturday. Number nine in race three.'

'Oh, is that good?'

'Well, I don't know what it means but race three has only eight runners.'

Gordon laughed and went out to the store room.

Hanging the daily on a rack next to a pile of glossies, I walked over to the doorway. As I went to leave, Angelique reached out and held my hand.

'Bill, you know you should talk to Bernard.'

'What about?' I said, wondering if she meant 'us', and wondered whether there was an 'us' and suddenly surprised I might have to confront my feelings for her.

'Oh, he is always saying since he came back here that the town is run by bottom feeders. So it may be better to start at the bottom rather than the top, don't you think?'

So, it was mundane real life, but a good point. Old Bernie knew a thing or two, which was why Angelique was so fond of him.

I pulled open the car door, sat and looked at the café door for a moment. Angelique was just flipping the closed sign to 'open' and I gave her a hopeful wave. She smiled and waved back with an open palm. I really should be more curious and ask more questions about the Bernie thing.

On my way back into the town, I called in at our house. Harry and I lived in an ageing bungalow near the business centre. Neither of us was that interested in the look of the place, so it had become a bit rundown. I mowed the lawns occasionally and Harry tinkered around with the paint work, so the weather boards were differing shades of white. Although I didn't smoke any more, I knew where I could find some dope. Harry hated it when I smoked dope after I left school and more or less kicked me out. Funnily enough, I didn't like it all that much but it helped to put up the wall between me, myself and the childhood I was leaving behind. The plastic bag had a few heads left. They were pretty dried up and stunk a bit. Some papers will still in the bottom of the bag and so I rolled a couple of smokes. I was about to leave when my phone went. It was Diana.

'Hey, where are you?'

'I'm here.'

'Ok. We need to talk about this story. Are you coming into the office?'

'Nah, not straight away.'

'Oh, okay so can we meet? Where are you going?'

'Well, I'm going to The Strand, the public bar. Not really your kind of place.'

'It's fine. I'll meet you there.'

The Strand was often full of holidaymakers during the summer but in winter it really was just another unfashionable seaside pub. Once upon a time you could see the harbour mouth from the bar, and watch fishing boats tie up along the wharf. Now the view was blocked by newer, taller buildings, including the post-modernist town council building. The Strand was today flanked by surf shops selling only clothes and the cafes that visitors, and some locals, tended to prefer. I'd usually park around the back in one of the pub's few car parks during the daytime. Wanting to ensure Diana knew where I was, I parked out the front and waited for a while. After what dad had told me, I wasn't too sure about Diana joining me for this visit. It wasn't so much that The Strand was a dump, which it kind of was, but the guy who I knew I'd meet there wasn't the sort you could count on for a welcome. Just sitting in the car I felt increasingly nervous about the prospect of meeting with George Joseph. He could greet you like, if not a long lost brother, at least a distant cousin. More often than not, however, he was twitchy and given to surliness, particularly if a deal was going on or he was in between fixes of whatever his poison was at the time. So I decided not to wait for Diana and got out of the car.

The rain had decided to join us again for the afternoon and arrived in a large gang in the space between the car and the pub door. Damn, I thought, another sloppy surf on its way. Poising at the door, I felt in my pocket for the joints then went in to the bar. Sure enough, George was standing at one of the leaner bar tables near the rear. Happy George or Angry George? It was hard to tell from his naturally surly disposition and the goatee that conspired against the air of respectability he was trying to achieve with his smart jeans and business jacket. He looked up and nodded as I came towards him, and actually smiled. Good, Happy George.

'Hi George, things going well?'

'Yeah, be better if I could figure this number out.'

'You're not doing the races are you?'

'Nah, Sudoku. I've got one box to go.'

One thing I should mention about George is that he was probably one of the cleverest guys around Coastlands, although a few cells may have been missing up top these days. He didn't really belong to a gang, well not so you would notice. It was pretty well known he associated with the big-time gangs, as well as some local smaller, fringe gangs. Balancing out these relationships meant George probably had the kind of skills that would have made him a diplomat in another life, if only he didn't end up dealing with final disagreements in a manner which had seen him spend a few lengthy spells away in the past.

Time was short, so I reached in to my pocket and quietly got out the joints.

'Feel like a smoke?' I asked, holding them closely in front of me so he could see them. George looked fleetingly over my shoulder but without flinching nodded and sipped his beer.

'What the fuck's this all about?' he asked, then jerked his head towards the back door of the bar. 'Hey Jos, I'm in the back office,' he called out to the woman behind the bar, who was stocking the fridge.

'This is a non-smoking establishment,' George added as he unfurled himself from his bar stool and headed out the back. He was a bigger guy when he stood up. I'd forgotten how imposing he could be even though he was not much taller than me.

George shoved his way through the back door of the bar. I followed him out on to the back steps overlooking the car park, the back of the takeaway bar next door and across the road to what passed for our local brothel, The Captain's Cabin.

'Welcome to wash and wank alley,' George said.

I lit the first joint after dampening it slightly. It was rough alright but I gave it him. He took a deep drag and refused to cough out but pulled the sort of face that said 'this really is bad shit'.

'Where'd you get this? The front lawn?' But he took another drag anyway and quickly burnt down the smoke, which wasn't hard as it was pretty dry. He handed me back what was left and rested his back on the rail over the steps.

'George, what do you know about the mayor?'

'Chill out Bill, why is there such a hurry? Enjoy the view.' He put a big bear arm around my shoulder and pulled me close. Waving his other arm around extravagantly he said 'One day, honey, all of this will be yours.'

He really did have the ability to be both menacing and cringingly funny at the same time.

'Well, I know you businessmen have a tight schedule, so your time's precious isn't it?' I said. It was true but maybe I was pushing it a bit. He grimaced slightly or it may have been a smile, and lifted his arm from around my shoulder.

'Yeah, well I'd heard you'd got in the shit with my mate, Mr Stead.'

We both had a chuckle at that.

'You know that's not hard,' I said.

'The mayor? Yeah, it's a strange one. No longer Brand new but Brand dead. Sex, drugs and rock 'n roll I reckon.'

'How do you mean?'

'Outside our little world, Bill, there are a lot of bucks in these three, so there's no reason why some of it shouldn't spill here,'

George said, nodding towards The Captain's Cabin across the road.

I was about to ask him to elaborate when he held up his hand. We could hear sirens coming down the Strand and cars pull up outside the pub.

'Looks like I've got another customer to deal with. You better get rid of that, fuck that's bad stuff,' he gestured to the remnants of the joint, which I flicked into the car park.

We turned to go back into the bar but before we opened the door, George looked through a small side window. Looking around his shoulder through the grubby glass I could see Stead and a couple of uniforms hassling the bar manager, her face stony. George grabbed me by the shoulder.

'Here give me that other smoke,' he said, pointing at my pocket.

'But...' I went to say.

'It'll give me something to talk about with Mr Stead.'

Stead was just heading away from the bar towards the back when we come through door. That song from Beirut popped into my head as Stead gestured to the two uniforms towards me.

'It's been a long time, long time since I've seen you,' I started to say as they grabbed me by both arms.

I noticed George just walked straight past him over to the bar where he ordered another beer and a packet of chips, propping himself up to watch proceedings.

Stead gave me a quick, winding tap to the midriff. He leaned down, his huge head and neck against mine.

'Turn out your pockets now, you little shit,' he said.

For some reason he nodded towards George, who just shrugged his shoulders. Stead plunged his hands into my pockets.

'If I find anything, I'll do you,' he said but was clearly frustrated.

'Hey,' I managed to squeeze out, 'shouldn't you be out looking for a killer instead of following me around?'

'Don't worry, I've got someone in mind for it, but this is an official police investigation and you've been banned.'

The uniforms let go at his nod. My guts were tied in a knot and hurt, but no worse than when I'd get hit by the slab of the surprise wave when surfing. Funnily enough my mind started drifting towards the waves and I saw a big surf pouring through. I squeezed my eyes shut tightly and shook my head.

'So you've got a suspect?'

'I didn't say that,' Stead said louder than was necessary. He shoved a finger in my face and was about to release a tirade when I heard a voice quietly behind his back.

'Hey Norm, we must stop meeting like this.' Diana was dressed in jeans and a jeans jacket, so she must have gone home to get suitably attired for a visit to the bar. Good Jimmyng, I thought.

'Hi Diana, Mr Stead and I were just have a little chat about a rather interesting case he's involved in at the moment.'

Stead's face was a picture of confusion, not knowing whether to lay a hand on me once again but quickly deciding it wasn't worth the trouble.

'Yes, I was just telling Mr Brown not to get in the way of an investigation,' Stead said, adding with the emphasis of shoving his face close to mine, 'or face a charge of obstructing police.'

Diana put a hand gently on his arm and said 'I'm sure it won't come to that now.'

Stead almost flinched and then relaxed. Gesturing to the uniforms, he strode over to the bar.

'Good Jimmyng Diana,' I said, while over her shoulder I could see George quietly lift a finger to his lips.

'I thought I should go home and change into something more suitable, so it looked like I arrived in time,' she said, and I looked closely at her broad, beautiful face and blue eyes. We turned to go and as we walked pass George, who turned back to the bar.

We went through the door. Sun. Rain water on the ground. Reflecting strange colours like shards of broken glass. Diana put her hand on my arm.

'Are you alright Bill? What on earth was going on in there?'

'You do have good Jimmyng don't you,' I said and let out a little breath that ended up in a quiet laugh.

'Mmm, yes, but what happened? What was Stead up to and who was that other character at the bar?'

'Well, Stead was just doing his usual thing of spraying it about a bit.' I turned around and looked back through the door and could see George and Stead huddled together in a corner down the back. The two uniforms were walking towards us with meaningful looks on their faces.

'There was nobody else.'

'Oh come on, stop playing games. You know what I mean.'

'If you say so,' I said, just as the two cops came through to door towards us. Diana's phone went with bird sound.

'Harry, yes. He's with me. We're on our way back. That's right. Yes, we've got a story to write.'

6

MR MARREN GOES FISHING

Police seek mystery suspect in Mayor's murder

by Bill Brown, Diana Macdonald and Neil Rabistock

A mystery stranger is understood to be at the centre of the manhunt for the killer of the Coastlands district mayor Bob Brand.

Police have placed a ban on providing The Coast Courier with information on the case following unauthorised disclosure of a photo of the murder scene.

However, we learned during a one-on-one meeting with Sergeant Norm Stead that police do have a suspect in mind.

No further information was forthcoming from Mr Stead, who was accompanied by two other uniformed officers during the visit to The Strand Hotel in downtown Coastlands.

During the police visit to the hotel, our reporter, Bill Brown, was searched by the officers and questioned by Mr Stead over this newspaper's own investigation into the mysterious death of Mr Brand.

We have learned that the district Mayor was seen shortly before his death on the outer part of the track at the Victory Racing Club.

One of our reporters saw him meeting with a tall, well-built man in a dark suit and sunglasses.

Although we have been unable to establish a connection between Mr Brand and the man, it is known that the racing club has been struggling financially as betting figures have dropped.

The racing club would not comment when approached by the reporter, Diana Macdonald, but issued a statement as follows: 'It is no secret times are tough for our industry. Bob Brand was a long-serving member of the Victory Racing Club Executive Committee and a respected member of the racing fraternity. Nevertheless we know of no reason why he should be killed for anything in connection with the club.'

Our civics reporter, Neil Rabistock, has combed the files of the Coastlands District Council and found some unusual aspects to recent dealings between the racing club and various council committees.

A number of matters have been held behind closed doors, with the public excluded. However, about six months ago, an item was included in the minutes of a promotional committee meeting from the town tourism board highlighting the impact of a closure of the Victory race track, should the club run short of funds.

Council officers approached refused to elaborate and the tourism board has told us the matter must remain confidential, even though it may have implications for Mr Brand's murder inquiry.

District Police Commander Steve Marren refused to comment on the speculation.

If you know any more, please email: info@thelastnewspaperintheworld.com

We were standing over Glen's desk looking at the front page. Included in the story was a small, rather grainy photo Diana had taken as she entered the bar, showing the hulking Stead standing over me and the two uniforms standing behind me. It was all a bit blurry but I guess it got the message across. Glen was a bit glum.

'It's a bit thin isn't it?'

It was more a statement than a question. Harry came through the door from his office.

'You lot, we're going to have visitors. Steve Marren's on his way, tidy this place up'

'Did he send you a message on the info email?' I asked.

'Not funny. Get this shit hole sorted out and get in here you lot.'

Glen went pale, and asked him what the Police commander wanted. 'He reckons we're interfering with their investigation and he wants to sort it out.' I moved some papers around my desk but I really didn't have too much of a mess. I glanced over and saw Neil deleting files off his system. Harry looked around and let out a sigh. 'Forget that. You lot had better come into my office, Glen, Bill, Diana, Neil. We'd better sort our shit out before these cops get here.'

Neil stopped deleting his files. Diana searched in her bag for a brush. She really didn't need to do anything. Her hair, even in the toxic light of the newsroom, seemed to shimmer. She had the jeans on again today, with a polo neck sweater probably a size too big.

'Bill,' Harry said. I hadn't realised he was looking intently at me. 'I've got a spare jacket in my cupboard. Brush your hair.' He jerked his head towards his office.

'What?'

'You want to look like you at least think you know what you're doing with these fellas.' I found an old tweed jacket in his cupboard. It wasn't too bad a fit. Harry handed me a comb from his drawer. 'Have a go at this.'

I looked at the small mirror on the inside of the cupboard door. Salt water and sun do something to hair, stiffening it and making it duller. Mine wasn't as bleached as it was during summer but it was still tough to straighten out.

'People pay big money to get a hair style like that B.B.' It was Diana. She and Neil came into the office carrying chairs, followed by Glen with a file of paper. At that point the comb was stuck in a particularly salty part of my scalp.

'What?'

'You know, that wild, unkempt look.'

Frustrated, I gave up and stood against the wall.

Harry was looking out the window.

'Right, they've arrived. I think you know how this is going to play out.'

I didn't have a clue but Neil did, saying: 'Yeah, they'll ask questions and we'll try to find out as much as we can, right.'

'I think they'll want some give and take,' Harry said, 'but each of you knows your angle. Neil, stay quiet about those documents you've got from the council but try to see if they give a glimmer of an idea what's gone down there. Diana, can you just watch what they say and how they say it.'

Dad looked at me and shook his head.

He looked into the office. I followed his gaze and could see Steve Marren entering, followed by Stead, Jimmy Tatua and a woman I hadn't seen before. 'Just behave yourself a bit, please,' Harry said quietly to me.

Going out of his office, he greeted his visitors, shaking hands with Marren, nodding at Stead and ushering the three into his office. Introductions all around, with Fish Marren noting that Jimmy had been appointed something called community liaison for the case and the new officer, Detective Inspector Judy Collingwood, had come from head office to oversee the investigation.

My phone beeped. It was a message from Diana. How did she do that without me noticing?

'Look @ stead' I had already and saw how he was staring straight at me, expressionless.

'Sorry about that. My library card's overdue,' I said, turning the phone off.

Harry and Fish both ignored me and were looking at each other.

'Shame about the weather,' said Harry, 'don't suppose you've had a chance to get out for some, fish.'

The police commander's already tight-fitting uniform seemed to grow slightly larger, before deflating slightly.

'Yeah, well, let's get down to business. You know what we're here for don't you? We are concerned that the line you are running in The Last Newspaper in the World is interfering with our investigation in the murder of the mayor. We realise the importance of the media and the role it must play. We thought we could reach some sort of accommodation with you so that you get what you want and we can make progress without your people,' looking at us standing against the wall, 'getting in the way.'

After saying this, Fish looked over to Judy Collingwood. She just nodded. He added, 'I am aware of the freedom of the press and this is in no way to be construed as police coming down on you to prevent you from doing your job.'

'Ah,' said Harry, looking over to Glen, 'couldn't agree more. You have your job and we have ours. The lines have become a bit blurred since you shut us out from your investigation.'

'With good reason don't you think?'

'Maybe, but that does mean we have run our own line doesn't it? Look, as an officer of the law you must know that the best defence is the truth. In this case,' Harry said looking at Stead, 'it is true that your Mr Stead told our reporter you did have a suspect, one of our reporters saw the mayor out at the race track with a mysterious visitor and there does seem to be something up with the racing club or at the least the land.'

'Yes, but if you start running around talking to potential witnesses it could impede any arrest and prosecution.'

'I understand that but I'm not sure how we can help. We do still have to get the news out.'

'Look, we seem to be going around in circles,' said Judy Collingwood. She had a surprisingly softly sophisticated voice for a senior officer. 'Shall we see if we can work together a bit better? Why don't you come back into the fold? We will share more with you and, likewise, you with us. Off the record, of course.'

Harry didn't say anything for a moment and in the silence I could hear the sound of a race caller on the radio over by the sports desk.

'Sounds good to me,' said Harry. 'So when's your next briefing?'

Collingwood looked over at her colleagues.

'The next one is at 9 o'clock tomorrow morning,' said Marren.

'Very good, we'll be there,' Harry said, rising from his chair. Handshakes all around and he and Marren exchanged invites for fishing trips that'd never happen.

While he saw them out, the rest of us stood about in his office wondering what to make of it. When he came back, Harry had a bit of a smile on his face.

'Well?' he said to Glen.

'So we're going to pull back from our own investigation and follow the police line then,' Glen said.

'Nah, I doubt it,' Harry said, he swore again and said something to the effect that there was no way he would let Stead get one up on us. For once, I was happy to hear dad swearing.

7

DIANA MEETS ANGELIQUE

'Bill, can you keep out of Stead's way for just one day?'

I nodded to Glen but added: 'Um, ah don't you think this has gone as far as it can go?'

Harry pursed his lips. 'What do you mean?'

'Well, you know, now that we're back in with the cops, why bother?'

More swearing, then 'You're the one who got us started on this. We can't just stop now because you're uncomfortable. We have a duty to continue our own lines for our readers.'

I heard Diana lightly chuckling beside me. I looked at Glen and he shrugged and gave me a 'don't ask bloody stupid questions' look.

'Right, Diana, I want you to go down to the police media briefing,' said Harry. 'You okay with that?' I looked around at her and saw she wasn't smiling but had narrowed her eyes.

'Neil is there any more to be gained from the council background reports?' Standing next to Diana, I realised how tall Neil was and how thin, his black trousers crunched around his waist by a narrow belt.

'Well, what I'd like to do is interview the people who are mentioned in those reports, either making decisions or just being on the committees.'

Glen and Harry looked at each other and nodded.

'Can you also see if you can find out anything about what's happening with the racing club,' Harry said.

'What about me?' I asked.

'I see the Americans have developed a jet fighter that can't be seen until it's blasted your arse off,' Harry said.

'Yeah, the Stealth bomber.'

'Beyond that even. That's not you though, is it?' Harry said, looking back at me.

I looked at Harry and thought how he knew very well I was the person who things happen to, good and bad.

'Look,' he said addressing us all, 'these sorts of crimes are usually about sex, drugs and rock and roll.'

'Yeah, that's what George Joseph reckons.'

'He'd know,' said Harry.

But Glen said: 'Harry, that's a bit simplistic isn't it?'

'Yeah but you know what I mean. The rock and roll in this case, I think, we've got a slight glimmer of through the various meetings. Bill what I want you to do is find out the sex and drugs part and how it ties up to the rock and roll.'

I squeezed my eyes shut and nodded.

'Ok, get out of here. I've got a newspaper to run.'

Sitting at my desk, trying to make a list. My hand was poised over a blank page. I could hear my computer humming as it looked after my stories and invited me to enter. I could see the beach stretching out in front of me, perfectly formed waves throwing themselves down. Just as I was about to rise and go for a surf, I saw Diana walk over to Glen. They looked at me and then Diana came over.

'Hey, let's go for a coffee and sort out what we're going to do.'

As we left the office, I saw Neil talking to Christine in the sports section. Diana started to walk down the road when we got outside but I called to her, 'hey let's go over to the beach.'

The surf wasn't quite as perfect as it had been in my mind's eye but nice lines still rolled through. Gordon's café was quite busy. Four or five people at tables pressed against the windows to make the most of the weak sunlight. Angelique greeted me with a smile, which she kept on as she looked at Diana.

'Bonjour Bill – your usual?'

'Of course.'

'And your girlfriend? What do you want?' she asked Diana.

'Angelique, this is Diana, she works with me.'

'Trim flat white for me please,' Diana said, smiling politely, because that's what she did.

'Of course, we girls must watch our weight, so difficult.'

Diana paid and we sat down at one of the small side tables, against the wall.

'Who is she?' Diana asked, looking at Angelique as she made our coffees.

'A friend. What did you think of our visitors?'

'Seemed a very reasonable request,' Diana said, pulling herself back a bit from the table and running a hand over her hair. I knew she was annoyed with me for avoiding her interest in my friend.

'Yeah, but do you think Harry is right? Should we continue with our own investigation?'

'Of course, why do you ask?' I looked at Angelique who was just finishing off our coffees and thought how I really loved her round face and the way her eyebrows curved fully over her eyes.

'Bill,' Diana said, gently waving long fingers in my face, 'why do you ask?'

'You know, aren't the police handling this really? Won't we just get in the way?'

'I think that's the point. No, just joking,' Diana said smiling, then saying more seriously, 'why, are you worried?'

'As Harry would say, my very good friend Stead seems to be after me on this, so I am a bit worried where it's going to end up, that's all.'

Diana was quiet and looked at me evenly. 'Where it's going to end up is we are going to get the story of our lives.'

'But doesn't that just piss off the cops?'

Diana, for all her university degree and clean, classic look, just shrugged.

'Coffee?' It was Angelique. She put the cups down and put a hand on my shoulder, proprietarily brushing my hair lightly with a hand first. 'Has he taken you to see Bernard yet?' she asked Diana.

'Bernard. Who's that?' Diana asked me.

'A friend.'

'Another friend. So should we go and see him now?'

Angelique gave me a gentle shove. 'You should. He knows more than you think.'

I knew that too but I hated the thought of facing Bernie feeling as I did about Angelique. Still, if anybody could tell me about the ins and outs of this town, it'd be Bernie.

'Sounds interesting,' Diana said, 'why don't we go now? Thanks Angelique.'

'Okay, just let me finish this first,' I gestured towards my cup, laughing now as the tension was released.

A small group of seagulls rose from the strip of grass outside Gordon's. Diana waved her arms in the air at them. 'Oh, go away. I hate birds don't you?'

'Not really. Why don't you like them?'

'It's those eyes and their little beaks.'

I was going to ask her if she'd ever poked a stick at a dead bird but decided against it. 'I suppose they can be a bit scary but I'm kind of used to them.'

We got in the car. Diana slammed her door shut.

'Careful,' I said, 'it's not that old.'

'Hmm, no.'

I don't think she was listening. As we started to drive down the beach road towards Bernie's place, she pulled a make-up kit out of her bag and looked into the small passenger side mirror on the visor. I was always a bit surprised looking at a woman applying her make up in these conditions. Living the kind of life that Harry and I did, make-up was not too common around the place.

'Watch the road, please,' she said, and I noticed I was drifting slightly towards the sandhills.

'We're just going to see old Bernie. I don't think he'd care.'

'Well, a girl's always got to look her best, as my mum says.'

I don't know if she'd actually applied anything as the winter sunlight reflecting off the ocean gave her face its own lustre.

'So how does your dad know Bernie?'

'Harry? Oh, something to do with the war.'

'Which one?'

'Vietnam, Bernie was a hero, I think. Somebody rescued somebody else but I'm not sure of the full story.'

'What about Angelique? Where does she fit in?' Diana asked, looking out towards the sea. We were turning into Bernie's place now, so I just said that was a good question.

'Something to do with Vietnam but I'm not too sure.'

'So she's French but from Vietnam?'

'Okay, let's go and do this.' The wheels crunched over what remained of shells scattered on the driveway. I pulled up near the back of the house.

As we got out of the car, Diana continued. 'It's okay, I understand why you like her. She's cute and exotic.'

'And a good friend.'

'*Mais oui*, let's go and visit friend Bernard.'

8

BERNIE READS THE MARKET

Bernie was sitting at a square dining table hunched over a laptop. He called out for us to come in when I knocked on the open back door. The wind had swirled some sand on the doorway but Bernie didn't seem to mind the weather. He waved us to come through the kitchen and into a small lounge. Propped against one wall was a large-screen TV. Rather than showing a sports event, the screen was tuned to a channel providing business news and stock indices. Bernie was dressed for business, even down to the tie and jacket. A visitor might think he had just popped in, or was on his way out, but I knew this was his daily ritual. Up and dressed for business, early into foreign markets and late out of local ones. He had a lean, tanned face and a head of hair that, while slightly greying, was sufficiently abundant to allow him to chuck some gunk into it to smooth it back. He took off his reading glasses and leapt up when he saw us come in. Well, that is, when he saw Diana, as he wouldn't normally worry about formalities with me, the son of his oldest and sometimes closest friend. Bernie normally would just grunt and point me to the kitchen with the instructions to put the kettle on for a cuppa. Unlike many men of his age, he'd be 60-plus, he didn't seem to have a 'thing' for much younger women. Of course, there was Angelique but their relationship was one loose end I had always had trouble tying up. 'The Colonel', as dad sometimes called him, did rise when he saw Diana.

'Well, my dear, what are you doing in the company of this rough sort,' he said, holding out his hand to her.

'So you're the famous Bernie,' Diana said and beamed, 'pleased to meet you.'

Through the wide lounge window I could partially see a perfect set forming over Bernie's shoulder as waves lined along the beach like soldiers coming to slowly to attention as they awaited their fate. The sandhills blocked my view as they broke but sea spray hung in the suddenly clear winter light.

'How are the markets?' I somewhat reluctantly asked. Reluctantly, because Bernie could sometimes get bogged down in detail, but it was his favourite thing at the moment.

'Very good. My gold stocks are really riding high right now. You should tell your dad to get into them, Bill. I've always said he could make more money in gold than his newspaper.'

'Probably, he's just got other things on his mind at the moment.'

'Of course,' Bernie said, frowning. 'Mayor Brand. I see you're stirring things along there.'

I thought about that for a moment. Was I 'stirring' as Bernie put it? It might have looked like that but I still didn't feel really engaged in the process. I shrugged, and told him how Angelique had suggested he might have some ideas for us.

'I don't know about ideas, just thoughts,' he said.

'Anything will help.'

'I could say I know only what I read in The Last Newspaper in the World, but that wouldn't be true, would it?' I looked over at Diana. She was staring intently at Bernie, probably wondering 'what's this dude on?', although she probably didn't quite use those words. I nodded and asked him to go on. It was his turn to pause and look out the window across the road to the sea. He took a deep breath and turned back to us. 'This is off the record, of course. You can use as much as you like but only as leads. Okay.' We agreed.

'You know Angelique. Why do you think she lives with me?'

'Because......,' my voice trailed off.

'Because, many years ago, on one of my trips to Vietnam, I met her mother. She was little more than a child herself. One of the chaps in our embassy there introduced me to her in a bar. Turns out she was controlled by a rather nasty fellow who specialised in peddling the very young to an ever-growing group of rather nasty foreigners. Her mum was almost past her use by date with this fellow, particularly since she now had a young daughter. Angelique's father was a French embassy official who had previously been in Cambodia, where he'd developed a taste for attractions of the young. By the time he got to Ho Chi Minh City, he'd lost all hope. Of course, he moved on quickly when Angelique arrived on the scene. Took his family to a posting in Mozambique, I think.'

Bernie paused for a moment.

'More coffee? Something to eat?'

We shook our heads.

'Please, go on,' Diana said quietly.

'While Angelique was a baby, it wasn't a problem. But there are some not very nice people about and it became a daily chore to prevent the little girl from going down the same road she had. It was almost expected that she would sell her daughter, as she herself had been sold. She resisted and eventually her man, growing tired of being the cat chasing the mouse decided: he would shift the mother on and keep the daughter. Place her in a bogus orphanage where she could be schooled and pulled out when required for special clients. All funded by aid money. He was a clever guy, I hate to say it. So we came up with a plan with my friend from the embassy. I would quietly, and quickly, adopt Angelique and he would open the way for the necessary clearances to bring her here. What would happen to her mum was more problematic. The idea was to establish the daughter here and then bring the mother out under the repatriation scheme. Really, though, her mother just wanted Angelique out of there. A brave woman. Ultimately, it may have cost her her life but really, I don't know. There was no contact. So that's how Angelique came here.'

Waiting for him to continue, I could hear the wind running through the fir trees at the back of his land, sounding like a giant combs sweeping back some troublesome hair. When Bernie didn't say any more, I asked: 'That's not all is it? What was the cost of this arrangement?'

Bernie looked up at me and laughed with raised eyebrows.

'Good question. Harry'd be proud. You're right, of course. There is always a price. In this case, I was banned from returning to Vietnam as the guy had connections in the government. That wasn't too painful, however, and as part of the deal with the embassy, our government asked me to quietly monitor paedophilia. So I received some small compensation for lost business opportunities by way of an early pension. Like I said, this is for your background only.'

'So as well as following the gold market...' Diana said.

'In the early days, I used to use my contacts during business trips into Asia. Produce a dossier once a year and that'd be it. Keep an eye out for our nationals indulging themselves. I once sat next to a former Qantas pilot on a flight to Bangkok. He was off to Vietnam and was happily extolling the virtues of villagers who would present them with a child bride. Now, of course, with the internet, all that has changed.'

'I bet,' I said, a little too sharply. 'Does Harry know about any of this?'

'Of course.'

'But you swore him to the old boys' secret?'

It was Bernie's turn to shrug. 'Good man your dad.'

Diana looked at me quizzically, and then shook her head.

'Sorry to ask, but what has all this got to do with Mayor Brand's killing? Was he mixed up in all this sort of thing?'

'I haven't quite been able to make that connection but we were close to it when he died.'

'We?' I asked. 'You mean you and Brand?'

'I suppose I do. When I read about plans to expand wash and wank alley, I thought I should have a quiet word with him.'

'Hang on, can you take that back a bit please Bernie?' I said, holding up my hand.

'Oh, sure, I thought I should have a quiet word with him and...'

'No just before that. You mentioned 'wash and wank alley'. Where'd that come from?'

'I don't know. It'd just come up in chatter I'd been getting and some of the links were suspicious, so I thought I'd see him on the quiet.'

'You haven't been talking to George Joseph, have you?'

'No, no,' Bernie rumbled, a line of his slick hair falling slightly ajar. 'Look, I've said too much already, and this is for your information only. For your background.'

I swore and said 'Bernic, this is infuriating, are we on the right track or not?'

'Steady old chap, now you're starting to sound like Harry. Put it like this: why would George Joseph be worried about the expansion of wash and wank alley?'

Diana and I looked at each other. 'Do you mean he's into prostitution as well as drugs?' Diana asked.

Bernie looked over at his screen. 'Oh, ah, the numbers are changing. One thing I've learnt from the financial markets is that you have to look at commodities from all angles. Push, pull; supply and demand; new entrants. That sort of thing.'

He started tapping and scrolling. I knew we had lost him then.

'Well, thanks a lot Bernie, we'll be going,' Diana said.

He waved at us without looking and said: 'Sure, sure, come back to me if you have any queries.'

Diana started to leave but I stood there with my eyes slightly shut and a bit of a grimace on my face.

'Bill,' Bernie said. He had turned to look up at me. 'I know this business isn't really your thing. You'd probably sooner be out there,' he said, gesturing with his head to the sea, 'but what we are talking about is important to this place and these people. Say hi to Harry.'

'Bill,' Diana called quietly, 'come on. Let's go back to the office.'

After a moment, I said: 'Thanks Bernie. I might need to come back to you, alright?'

Bernie nodded, looked at Diana and said, 'It's been a pleasure,' and focused on the screen.

9

EMILY'S PENCIL FACE

Diana and I went out through the small lounge on to the back step.
I hadn't noticed it had begun to rain again. I just wanted to grab
my board from the back of the car and run across the road into the
sea. Throwing my keys to Diana, I got in the passenger's side.
Diana adjusted the seat and the mirrors, pausing a moment to
look at herself. I smiled at the ritual. We drove down the driveway,
the shells glistening in the rain and crackling as the car rolled
slowly over them. In the car, I couldn't smell the sea but I could
sense it, so I dropped the window down a bit. Some rain came in
and wet my face. I could taste the salt spray in the drops.

'Please put the window up. It's getting wet,' Diana said as we
turned into the road. 'Is that why you wanted me to drive? So you
could stick your head out the window and get the car wet?'

What I had been really thinking was that I'd get Diana to drop
me off so I could cop off for a surf. Let my mind do its own work
on what Bernie had told me. Maybe go for a coffee with Angelique.

'I might just get you to stop up here by the store.'

'What? Why?'

'Just thought I might go for a quick surf.'

Diana looked over at me, her face made up in a way that told
me she was sceptical.

'No, forget that. We have to get back to the office. There's a lot
to talk about.'

I was quiet.

'Besides, you can catch up with Angelique later.'

'It's just I've got a lot to think about and I can't do that in the office, with all that noise.'

'Sorry Bill, that's the job. Let's see where this story goes first shall we?'

She looked over at me and I gave her the upward tilt of my chin that is the local version of 'affirmative'.

We drove by the store and turned up the hill back to town. I could see Angelique behind the counter. We had a lot to talk about, or maybe sometimes there are things you can't talk about.

'So what did you make of Bernie?' I asked, hoping to swerve the conversation away from Harry and me.

'He does know a lot that he isn't saying,' Diana said, changing gear as we wound over a particularly winding stretch of the hill.

'Obviously.'

'And he's a bit of a drama queen isn't he.'

'Maybe. I don't know.'

I looked at Diana as she drove along. She was totally focused on the story in a way that I was unable to at that moment, picking apart the pieces and put them back together so they made sense.

'You do know what Bernie told us was on background, so...'

'Oh, of course, but it is where we take it that matters. It's how we connect Mayor Brand's murder to whatever it is. Is it a paedophile ring? Or is there more?'

'Sex, drugs and rock 'n roll,' I said.

'What do you mean?'

'It's something that Glen said.'

'Well we've got the sex, so do you think there're drugs involved? And what's the rock 'n roll?'

We decided, well I suggested, we wait until we get back to the office before going any further. I really just wanted some quiet. Turning the sounds on instead, I heard Amy Winehouse singing one of her B-side tunes, *Best Friends*. Something about her best friend knowing all her faces and being the person she most liked to smoke it up with. I turned it off.

'You're not going to stick your head out the window again,' said Diana, smiling at me.

I laughed and told her it was all good and, yeah, I was just thinking about the story.

When we arrived back into town we parked the car outside the office behind an old Chrysler, black with fins.

'Look at this monstrosity,' Diana said.

I'd seen it. I knew who it belonged to and wondered why it was parked outside The Last Newspaper in the World.

As we got out of the car, I saw Emily Lewis coming around the back of the Chrysler. She was taller than me, dressed totally in black, with a long black, hippy skirt. She was always slim in that athletic way. She was much slimmer now and her face had grown tighter, her features more pinched. I hadn't seen her much since we left school but I had passed her by when walking through the weekly market on The Strand recently. Emily was with a heavy-set man, hanging on to his arm. His face was kind of obscured, like somebody had used a pencil to scrawl across his features. So he didn't have a blank look, he just didn't have a look. Except for his eyes, which peered through the scribble with the kind of blank look I thought you might see on somebody before they cut your throat. I quickly turned away, but before I did I noticed Emily had an air almost of somebody in ecstasy. Her thin lips had a fixed smile and she seemed very secure, very protected. This wasn't always the case with Emily. Although I didn't know too much about her background, most of us knew it wasn't a happy family equation. As I said, she was a good athlete but she did tend to lose it during or after events. Tripping up opponents during races, then fighting them to the ground when they complained afterwards meant the prizes she should have won were snatched from her grasp. Suspensions from school inevitably followed such incidents and, as her school work suffered, she drifted further and further away to another world. The Last Newspaper in the World carried a report a while ago that she had been sentenced to two years in jail for defrauding a local retailer. Emily mustn't have served the full two years, because her she was, standing in front of me, almost towering over us.

'Bill, hiya, howyagoin, whatchadoin, workin for the old man now, eh?' Emily's eyes darting back and forth between me and Diana. 'Why don't ya introduce me to your girlfriend?'

'She's not my girlfriend,' I said, possibly a little too quickly. 'This is Diana, we work together. Diana, this is Emily. We were at school.'

Diana nodded watchfully, saying nothing. Emily looked excited or amused.

'You should grab him while you can. Do you know our Bill was a real star at school,' Emily said. At least she didn't use the simpering complaining voice that used to be the prelude to a blow up.

'A shooting star?' Diana asked. I didn't hear but I just knew she was laughing quietly.

Emily blinked quietly then turned to me.

'I've got some news for you,' she said and jerked her head away.

Turning to Diana, I nodded. When I turned back, Emily was already striding towards her car. I climbed in and closed the heavy black door. She gunned it and we lurched away from the curb. We didn't drive far, just down to The Strand and turned into what George had called 'wash and wank alley', before going into the tar sealed car park behind The Captain's Cabin. I shouldn't have been surprised to see she worked at the brothel, but I was. When I said so, she laughed.

'Nah, not really. Guys don't really go in for the scrawny type. They come here to follow their dreams not to visit somebody who looks like their missus. I do fill in some times when we are caught short or have a rush on. But mostly I help James. I think you've seen him.'

Oh, so 'Pencil face' was a brothel owner, I thought.

'So yeah and I am the duty manager when he's not here.'

That made sense also. Not too many people would give Emily trouble.

We climbed the stairs and entered through the back door, going down a hallway into a foyer through which I could see the street front. 'Pencil face' was sitting at a large table, staring at a laptop.

'Welcome to The Captain's Table. What is your desire?' he said in a monotone without looking up.

'Sweetie, this is the guy I was telling you about,' Emily said, her voice going up a pitch into a kind of coo.

He looked up at me and I swear I could see the pencil lines moving as his face sketched itself into an expression of slight interest, indicated by the line of his right eyebrow lifting slightly.

'Bill, this is James. James, this is Bill Brown, you know my friend from school.'

Friend was going too far but it was a delicate moment, so I let it slip by.

'B.b? Does that make you the smallest gun then?'

'Something like that.'

'So why are you here? What can I do you for newspaper guy?' James said, picking up and putting on a captain's cap.

'James, you know I've told you, you know about this business with the mayor. Please honey, maybe Bill can help,' Emily said, as she wrapped her arms around his neck and pushed her body close into his back.

Out of nowhere, I had become that guy, the newspaper guy, somebody who would be expected to listen with avid interest to people's stories. Suddenly, I wanted to say 'don't tell me your story; I don't want to hear about your sordid world or your crummy life, must go, time for a surf'.

'What's the story?' I heard myself say, thinking now of Harry back at the office, Glen and the crew.

The pencil ran over James's face and sketched what could either have been a wry smile or a grimace.

'I hear you're a live and let live kind of guy,' James said, pushing himself back from the table and shrugging off Emily. 'Now's as good a time as any, before we get busy.'

He wrapped a hand around Emily's waist, told her to bring some tea.

'Not what you expected? The tea I mean. You need your head in this business and with these girls. Well, I say girls but it's a long time since any of them has been that. Twots on legs is what I'd call them.'

He looked directly at me, his face scribbled as I almost saw the artist's pencil move side-to-side.

'The Mayor, Mr Brand. What's that all about?' He leaned forward to me as I sat opposite.

'Sex, drugs and...'

'Rock 'n roll. Yeah I've heard all that before. You're right about the first two, but there is no rock 'n roll here just a bunch of crap. Bad crap.'

Emily brought in a tray with a pot of tea, cups and saucers and milk and biscuits.

'I'll be mother,' she said, which caused both James and me to smile.

A cup almost disappeared in one of James's hands.

'You'll scribble whatever you fucking want but no quoting me, right?' James said, the pencil sketching its way over his face again.

I blinked at him and took a sip of strong tea.

'Sure, sure. Not a bad brew Em.'

10

AT THE CAPTAIN'S TABLE

After telling Emily she was in charge of the table, James signalled me to follow him. We went through a side door in the foyer and trudged single file up a narrow staircase. The steps were wooden with worn black paint. A narrow side window lit our way. At the top, we went through a door into what looked like an attic converted into a store room. Cartons of accessories were stacked on one side and shelving on the other held essentials, such as bedroom and bathroom supplies. Beyond the stores, a square cast iron outdoor table stood in front of a large industrial window complete with thickened security glass. A large beach umbrella was opened above the table. James walked over and put his tea down on the table, taking a wrought iron chair to one side and nodding for me to take the other.

'I don't get out much, so Emily got me this over summer,' James said, taking a sip of his tea and leaning back. He really was a solid guy and I wondered how the puny chair could take the strain.

'I wondered.'

'She's good like that. This is my get away place.'

I must have signalled a query, because he added: 'You know what it's like working with chicks. Don't get me wrong, they're good earners but a shitload of trouble.'

My face said I sympathised with his plight. Below I could see The Strand stretching out towards the harbour. I could see the top of the building housing The Last Newspaper in the World. Above, clouds started to peel back soft, almost feminine layers to show a pale sky. I got out my pad and found a pen below it in a side pocket.

'Nice view,' I offered, hoping to get James talking.

He didn't follow my gaze but was staring at me intently. The eyes narrowed.

'So what do you know?' he asked.

My first thought was damn. It was going to one of those, where sources want only to know what you know without you knowing what they know. I let out a low breath, almost relieved at not learning more than I needed to know.

'Well, not as much as you I guess,' I offered.

'That'd be right but you guys never print everything you know.'

It was my turn to nod in the affirmative.

'Well, we've the picture it's tied up with a land deal, along with maybe the sex trade and possibly drugs of some sort.'

James shifted his bulk around in the tiny café chair and looked out the window.

'How do you think this place came to be here?'

I shrugged, knowing the laws allowed brothels to be established.

'Usual story, I suppose, you apply and get approval from the council? Wouldn't that be pretty straightforward now?'

'You'd think so, wouldn't you?'

At this point I was trying to recall details of the hearings surrounding the council hearings. I guess I wasn't paying attention at the time, because it all seemed pretty vague. I could recall something about local community and religious groups expressing concerns, but in our complacent way it all came to nothing.

'Yeah, there was some opposition wasn't there? It came to nothing much, though?'

James looked at me with a little line of frustration running through his eyes. I was obviously a bit of a let-down as a reliable witness as far as he was concerned.

'Do you remember the mayor came out in support? Big help he was at the time.'

'So you're saying you got the mayor on side to help you set up your operation here? Why'd that get him a bullet through the middle of the forehead? Why now? Wasn't this more than a year ago?'

Suddenly I seemed interested. James even realised this as his mouth arranged itself into a close approximation to a suitably pleasant grimace.

'It's not the time but the Jimmyng. Do you think we're makin' money?'

'Well, you're still here but it'd be seasonal wouldn't it?'

'Could've been but for the harbour expansion.'

Now I recalled how about the same time as James was getting his little operation off the ground, the mayor had successfully pushed through a long-delayed plan to expand the harbour to allow in larger, offshore fishing boats and ocean-going pleasure craft. Even during winter more foreign fishing crews used the harbour as a stopover, and there did seem to be more luxury boats coming and going.

'Are you saying the mayor was shot because he pushed through the re-development of the harbour? Seems a bit extreme.'

'Nah, I'm not saying anything like that but I helped Mr Brand with his pet project and he helped me with mine. Don't ask,' James said to hurriedly head off the obvious follow up.

'Why do you think George Joseph is spending more time sitting in the pub talking to your cop mate Stead?'

'Could be all sorts of reasons but I suppose you're going to tell me they're the best of friends.'

My phone vibrated in my pocket. Harry must be getting impatient, again. I ignored it.

'Best friends, no, but they are both worried about the same thing. The same as me but I don't have as many friends as George.'

'But maybe you have the same enemies?'

James nodded and stood up. I tapped my fingers on the table, telling myself to stay focused. Rain was falling heavily now. Out at sea, whitecaps licked the top of waves. The harbour mouth was still open thanks to the large new breakwater and other works, whereas in the past it would have closed out.

'Look, the mayor, my friend, gets a hole in the head. Do you think I'm worried? You bet. Your mate George is worried too and even Stead. Opening up the harbour has been good for my business, don't get me wrong, but I'm not into kiddy smuggling and I guess George isn't too keen on the heavy stuff.'

'Methamphetamine? P? I thought any of that coming here came down from Auckland, via the gangs?'

'Sure, look at that down there,' James said, point down at the harbour.

My outdoor chair scraped on the floor as I pushed it back and stood up to join James looking out the window.

'Big trawlers, pleasure boats from all around the place, even overseas. Not bad for a quiet little dump like this,' James said.

There was a knock and Emily stuck her head around the door.

'You've got a visitor. A cop. That guy Stead.'

James nodded without taking his eyes off me and said: 'You were talking to me about new directions in the town's tourism sector, right?'

'Yeah, that'll do it.'

We went down. Stead was standing with his two uniform pals. Who else? He even had his mouth twisted into half a smile when he saw me. I nodded at him and went straight out the front door.

'Hey you, stop,' I heard as I started down the road.

Turning, I saw Stead's chin staring down at me.

'So are you going to tell me what you were talking about or am I going to have to read it in the paper?'

'Probably, sure, but I think you know all about it anyway.'

Stead looked at me like he was going to dip into the pool of his anger again, but the feeling eased.

'Yeah, that's right,' he said. 'Surprised to see you are familiar with places like this. I didn't think it was your style.'

I wondered what my style was and how did he know, or care, anyway.

'You aren't going to get anyone for this murder are you?'

'No comment.'

We looked at each other in silence for a moment, before Stead turned and walked back into The Captain's Table.

I went back to The Last Newspaper in the World and we put together a story.

11

OFF TO THE RACES

There are times when I feel like I'm falling through the floor. I heard that on one of the soaps Harry was secretly watching one night. Secretly, because he pretended to criticise them but he really was hooked, the poor old guy. Harry wasn't that fussy what he watched but I recall one of the characters say 'I was so embarrassed, I felt like falling through the floor'. Don't even remember the programme really. I just remembered the phrase when I was sitting at my desk in the newsroom at The Last Newspaper in the World. One moment I was looking over into the office where the sun was lightly falling on the back of Harry's head. His balding head was down as he scrolled down a page. It looked casual but I knew he was scanning the words with the thoroughness of a laser. Probably more efficiently, as he would not only be able to recite the contents but also spit out an analysis of what he had read. As I sat watching him, bathed in sunlight, I started to fall into the floor, swallowed up by my own thoughts. Then a shadow blocked out the light.

Looking up I could see it was the racing reporter, Christine Dobson. She was out of her track gear and into a still casual but dressier outfit.

'Hi, ah, are you going somewhere?' I asked.

She smiled, which must have been a bit hard because she had a cold sore on her bottom lip no doubt picked up while attending early morning horse training gallops at the local track.

'We are going somewhere,' Christine said.

I gently shook my head and looked at her. Behind the lips her face was tanned the way of outdoors people. Hers was not as hard as some, however. She too shook her head, her ponytail falling forward.

'Yes, Bill, you're coming with me to the races in Rotovegas.'

'What, why does it take two of us to do that?'

'It's not my idea I can tell you. Harry seems to think you should take some pics for me.'

She blinked and smiled. 'I don't know why. I usually take the pics. You'll have to ask him,' Christine said, flicking her head back towards Harry's office.

I shrugged. 'When are we going?'

'Now,' she said, and when I looked surprised, she added, 'It's already getting late.'

I looked over at Harry's office. His head was still down, wading through the paper in front of him, but he looked up briefly and glanced over at me. As I almost got up to go and see him, his head went down sharply. I wanted to ask him why he was sending me to another town, where his newspaper didn't go, to take pictures of horses. Shouldn't I have been trying to dig around and find more on the Mayor Brand murder? After all, this seemed a good time to try to have another look at the murder.

'Harry said I had to tell you to get a really good pic of one of Pat McComb's horses. It's running in the third.'

'In those exact words?'

'Not exactly; he does get worked up doesn't he,' Christine said, but not too seriously.

I closed my eyes and tried to think what, if any, connection there might be between horse racing and Mayor Brand's murder.

'Everything alright?' It was Harry. I looked around and saw Christine grabbing her gear off the desk.

'Sure, why not. I'm going to Rotovegas to take a pic of your old mate's horse, right?'

Harry nodded.

'And...?' I asked.

'And I thought it'd be good for you to get out of town for the day. Chat to some racing people.'

'And Pat?'

'Yeah, and Pat.'

Pat had told me something about a land deal and the local racing club at the time of the murder but this never went anywhere.

'So you think he knows more than he told me?'

'Could be,' Harry said, and shrugged. That was scary. I think I had made the same gesture a few minutes ago. 'Either he does or somebody in that circle does. Here.' He handed me a small roll of notes. 'Have a few bets but make sure you shout Pat a few whiskeys.'

'Pretty crude isn't it?'

Again, the shrug.

'Are we ready?' asked Christine as she joined us.

'Yes, but take him around home first so he can put some decent clothes on,' Harry said, and when I closed my eyes and shook my head again, he added: 'Just grab a jacket and a tie. Looking like a surfer dude might be okay around here but you are representing the newspaper.'

We drove around to the place where Harry and I lived. He was probably right when he said it'd do me good to get out of town for the day. Christine told me to be quick as we were going to miss the first race at least. I left Christine in the lounge surrounded by our debris. It looked a bit like a scene from a battle between books and magazines with newspapers having their own war zone. I grabbed a shirt with a collar but couldn't find a tie, so went into Harry's room where his closet was nicely stacked with ties dating back to the 1990s and even the 1980s. I resisted the wider, satin look and managed to find a narrow tweed tie.

'Bill, come on, how're you doing? We have to get a move on,' Christine called from the lounge.

I hesitated for a moment, remembering it had once been filled with the clothes of my grandmother, who died not long before Harry picked me up from my parents in Auckland. Returning to my room, I picked up a Billabong full-zip hoodie from where it had been residing over the back of my dresser. Unused for a while, I knew Harry didn't like the casual jacket that much but he wasn't going to Rotovegas.

We got in the car. Christine driving, and me in the passenger seat preparing for a sleep. Some marketing guru had told Harry it would be a good idea to promote the newspaper on the car.

Instead of the usual fresh paint job and a logo, Harry had an image of one of our more colourful front pages covering the car from bonnet to boot. The Last Newspaper in the World masthead was wrapped around the middle. We'd gotten used to the looks and decided to put up with it as it was one of Harry's few extravagances.

When we went over the bridge out of town I could see the river running quite brightly. It was a clear, if windy day, although I could see some clouds in the distant hills where we were heading. I closed my eyes again and fell asleep. I awoke to Christine shaking my shoulder and my phone humming out an alert. I fought back the temptation to answer it but neither Christine nor the phone would let up.

'It's the office,' I said, 'probably Harry with last minute orders.'

She laughed but thought it would be a good idea for me to answer it. I wasn't so sure.

We were nearly in the hills now. I returned Harry's call but as it started to go through I pressed end call.

'What's that? Is your connection breaking up? It should be alright from here,' Christine said, looking up the highway.

I looked away at the bush on the surrounding range starting to wrap around us.

'I don't know. It's not a good signal.'

'Still, must be nice for you to get out of the office for a day. I don't know how you can stand it, being inside all day. That's why I love my job. Okay there are those early starts when I have to go to the track or cover a kids' sports event.'

She looked enthralled and I was suddenly aware of how Harry was providing the kind of life Christine might have struggled to find elsewhere at home. It was probably true for some of the others at least. Christine's interest and excitement in her work contrasted with my own lack of joy. Maybe, because I was the owner and editor's grandson, I was less than excited about the whole business. I was fully involved in reporting the unfortunate death of Mayor Brand; almost too involved some might have suggested. Looking over at Christine driving us around one of the lakes towards a day's work at a rainy racetrack, I envied her, her obvious glee at the day ahead and thought 'I must try harder'.

'What are you looking at?' she said as she flicked on the

windscreen wipers, before braking as we came into a corner around one of the lakes.

12

AMBER'S GOLD

Dreams come from the strangest places. As Christine nudged the car around the bends to the lakes on our way to Rotovegas, I fell asleep. I dreamed I was walking along the water's edge with Angelique. Holding hands, bliss-filled as the water streamed in from a small surf at the beach. As we walked, I could feel the current pulling at our shins but when I looked over I saw Angelique was submerged up to her neck in still water. When I looked down hurriedly I saw that I too was neck-deep. I sensed the water smelled less than fresh, but can you smell in dreams? Looking back at her, I saw Angelique was again stepping through the freshness of a sea surge. Looking down I could see water wrapping around my feet as the tide pulled away. Letting go of Angelique's hand, I turned and ran into the sea's incoming waves. She laughed. The sun shone.

I awoke to a steady rain fall and the rotten eggs smell that is Rotovegas's signature.

'It always rains on race day at Rotovegas,' Christine said as an attendant in a white coat waved us through to the official parking area.

'How do you do it?' I asked her. 'You know, come out to dumps like this on days like this?'

We pulled into a parking space on the grass adjacent to the race track. Christine reached over to the back to pull over her bag bulging with race-reporter gear – the binoculars, the form guides, pads, pens, and pencils for the wet. She was close to me as she leant over and turned so she was right in my face.

'I could ask the same question of you Bill. How do you go out into the storm sea just to surf some crummy waves?'

I'd forgotten I'd seen her riding her horse at low tide along the beach one recent morning. She was all business now as she quickly checked the contents of her bag, and then looked at me.

'Right, you know what we're going to do?' Christine said, suddenly in charge.

'Yep, Harry wants me to get a pic of Pat McComb and his horse.'

'For some reason.'

'For some reason,' I said and nodded.

'Okay, why don't you stay with me until we find Pat and take the pic.'

We exchanged phone numbers. I pulled the camera bag out. The rain seemed lighter than it had felt in the car. We heard the announcer calling the three minute warning to the start of race two. We ran through the rain, showed our passes to another attendant outside the members' only part of the stand. The rain stopped as we climbed the stairs to the front of the stand. I could see the horses being loaded into the barrier on the far side of the track.

'Is there something from home in this race?' I asked Christine as she took in the race start through her binoculars.

'Nah, I just wanted to see you running.'

I turned around with my back against the rail and looked at the crowd in the stand. Well, it was almost a crowd. Harry obviously hadn't been to the races for a long time, at least not a midweek meeting in Rotovegas. I think I was the only guy with a tie on in the whole place, apart from a few official looking men. The stand was split in two, with members, trainers and assorted types on the side closest to the finish line and the paying public on the other side. It made for an unusual feeling of living in a semi-detached with neighbours who were the same as you but different only because of the ticket you had slung around your neck. Near where we stood, a young couple sat watching the race intently, the guy holding a baby in one arm as he urged his horse on with the other. Over the barrier, a group of young women had dressed up for the occasion, one or two even going so far as to adopt the fascinator hat-style more used to metropolitan cup days. They were in their delightful fantasy, smiles on their faces as they cheered and held up glasses. We are having fun at the races, midweek, midwinter, in Rotovegas.

'Come on,' Christine said, nudging me. The horses were coming back to the birdcage after the race. As we left the stand she pointed up the top of the stairs where cameras were televising the event and told me to look up there or down below around the birdcage if I wanted to find her later.

'You really are a watcher aren't you?' she said to me as we walked across pavement to the horse stalls behind the stand. Trying to avoid puddles, I agreed with her.

'You know you need to get a life Bill.'

'What do you mean? There's nothing wrong in taking an interest in people around you.'

'That's not what I mean and you know it. You might've been looking at sparrows balancing on a branch.'

I shrugged, again.

'Oh, there's Pat,' Christine said pointing to a stall where Pat was making final preparations for his horse to be led out.

'Hey 20 cents, are you winning?' I called out. Pat looked up sharply on hearing his old nickname being called out but he smiled when he saw us and came over to the fence. Like most of the others, he was casually dressed with a course bib pulled over his wet weather gear. He gave the horse a pat on the neck.

'Harry said you might come. I must be going to win today,' Pat said as we shook hands. 'Don't quote me on that,' he said, turning to Christine.

'We do need to get a pic of you and your horse in action,' she said.

'Okay but after the race. I've got to go and take him around to the birdcage,' he said, gesturing towards the horse stall.

'Haven't you got a groom to do that for you,' I asked, observing most of the other trainers sending off youngsters to guide their horses around to the front of the stand.

'Usually, but not today. It's not worth it with just one horse here.'

A tiny attendant read out numbers as the horses were led out through a gate.

'27/7, 15/7, 12/7, 24/7,' he called as he checked out the brand number and the age of the horses.

'So these are all three year olds, right?' I said to Christine as Pat took his horse through the gate.

'Right, and Pat must think it's got a chance to bring just one horse here today, even though it's not done much.'

'What's the name of Pat's horse again,' I asked Christine as we walked back to the stand, our gait slightly faster. I stopped at the TAB counter to put on a bet before we went through to the birdcage.

'Quite the big time punter aren't you,' Christine said as she saw me putting $10 for a place on Amber's Gold.

'Yeah, what do you think?' I looked over and she smiled, then turned and walked through to the birdcage. The horses were filing in by this stage and jockeys came out from under the stand. The colours of the silks gave the area something of circus feel on this dull provincial day. I half expected them to start doing somersaults and back flips, or maybe build a pyramid in the cheerleader style. But the other half knew many of them had starved themselves and manipulated their bodies to reach the weight and retain the strength needed to ride their mounts. Then again, maybe they were like cheerleaders. Male and female riders were virtually indistinguishable, their small frames upright as they strode forward to spring on their mounts. Some exchanged banter with owners and trainers whose wishes most would be forced to ignore in the course of their work. Pat legged up a jockey who had looked like a kid who wanted to go back to bed when listening for his instructions. On board now, his eyes suddenly widened as he guided Amber's Gold into line with the others making their way out on to the track. The announcer called the horse's name, including the information that he was being ridden by a local wonder boy who had been making a name for himself around the tracks. I looked over at the screen showing win and place estimates. Amber's Gold had been at $15 to win when I had put my bet on and $4.60 for a place. Now he was down to $9 and $3.20. I looked over and saw Pat was talking a guy who looked like a

Chinese cowboy, wearing a smart winter jacket and tight jeans tucked into expensive boots. They turned away and walked up the stairs into the stand. Pat saw me as he went by but just gently shook his head and continued on.

'That'll be the owner,' Christine said. I gave a little start, as I had been engrossed in my thoughts.

'Oh, yes of course. Do you know him?'

'No, not really. Come on, I'm going up to watch the race but I want you to go down by the fence with those other photographers, just in case.'

'Okay, I've got to do something first.'

'Don't you dare miss this race, and look for Pat's green and gold colours,' Christine called after me as I headed through the stand to the tote. A queue had grown since I put my place bet on and suddenly I found my nerves winding upwards. I added $5 to win on the bet and hurrying back to the birdcage I started assembling my camera, adding a longer lens for luck. The announcer was just going through his patter like a hip-hop dance leader winding up his crew as the final horses were entering the starting gate. It all seemed very orderly.

13

A MUDDIED TRACK

Two other photographers leaned against the fence near the starting line. Both had one camera with a large lens at the ready and another slung around their necks. I felt a bit underdone with my single camera and not-so-long lens. At least I had a good digital and a sharp lens. I tried to figure out the best angle for a shot but really I was just fiddling around. It can be quite quiet on a race course when you are away from the crowd, or when you are thinking about something else. I turned around and looked up into the stand. A few people were climbing quickly up into their seats. I could see Christine at the top of the stairs. I think she was looking at me and pointing to the starting gate. I heard a click and turned around.

'You won't see much looking that way,' said the woman next to me. She had an open face, with brown hair tied into a sporting pony tail. I guessed she must have been local as she was wearing a ski jacket to keep out the cold. I shivered involuntarily.

'Which media are you from,' she asked, looking towards the gates as the last horse was loaded in.

'The Last Newspaper in the World, over on the coast.'

'What the heck are you doing here on a day like today?'

'I wish I knew myself,' I said, but was drowned out as the gates opened and the race caller wound his voice into his work.

Twelve hundred metre races can be a big race for three-year-old horses. Not quite like first day at school, that's more the two-year-olds, but more like little kids trying to be big kids. As it was, I didn't see the first 200 metres because I was thinking about what Harry really wanted me to do here. Then I looked up and could just see the horses on the fair side of track. They seemed to be running in slow motion, going up and down like they really were at a circus, but as they approached the straight their speed increased. Amber's Gold was somewhere near the front and wide. I noticed the woman next to me was tracking the field with her big grey lens, looking like she was going to blow them away with a great shot. Just as I adjusted my position on the fence rail, the horses swung into the straight. People were calling for their favourites but the names were all entwined like the rope of hope. I got the field into focus and tracked them forward as they quickly ran down the distance. Suddenly the little horses were racing very fast.

'Where's Amber's Gold; I can't see Amber's Gold,' I called, swinging the camera back and forward.

'Wide. On the outside.'

I steered my camera down the rails and saw Pat's horse charging down the outside straight at me, leading by several lengths. Mud flew up from his hooves. I swung around and holding the camera above my head kept shooting as Amber's Gold galloped past. I fell on my back. The other photographers gave me that loser look and the woman shot off a quick pic before I could scramble back up. I quickly checked my shots. They were mostly all a blur but there was a really nice one. The jockey was smiling a sleepy smile as they hit the finish line and Amber's Gold seemed to be winking directly at the camera. Harry'd like that, I thought.

As I straightened myself out, I felt spits of rain and turned my face to the sky. Then I just about fell over again, as Christine arrived and gave me a surprisingly hefty shove. I looked around and she grabbed my arm, giving my back a healthy slap as she brushed me down.

'At least tell me you've got a decent pic somewhere in there,' she said, smiling but angry at the same time. I showed her the sequence.

'Nice pic but I can't see the finish line. Hmm, it'll have to do. Come on, let's at least get a shot of them coming back.'

The placegetters were filing back into the birdcage now and Christine pushed me forward to take a pic of Amber's Gold and the jockey saluting the crowd. As Pat came down to the winner's chute, I slipped around the barrier and picked him up talking to the jockey and stroking the horse. Christine chatted to him and took some notes. As he was about to lead the horse away to the stalls behind the stand, I asked him if we could have a drink later.

'Sure. Where?'

'Up in the bar. I'll shout you a whiskey if you like,' I said, pointing at the grandstand.

'Nah, I don't do that anymore,' Pat said as he turned to lead the horse away.

'Well where then?'

He nodded over at the cafeteria. I guess it really had been a long time since Harry had been to the races.

Christine said she was going to catch up with some friends and we could meet up after the next race. I said that suited me fine and headed around to the tote to pick up my winnings. Not a bad return for a lazy punt. It was raining quite heavily, so instead of walking over to see Pat working on Amber's Gold, I went into the lounge area and worked on my phone. The beach web cam was pretty obscured but I could see a nice swell building up underneath a low sky. Suddenly, I wanted to get out of there, go home, and go to the beach. The sea was clean even when it was filled with seaweed and rubble washed down in winter storms. Looking around, the race course seemed grimy, claustrophobic, the people mundane and even the usually comforting green expanse of the race track like a giant corral.

I spotted Pat coming in and waved him over. We got something to eat – me a hot dog and Pat a salad bun. Tea and coffee was self-service and free. I offered to pay for the tea and coffee; it was the least I could do. As we sat down, Amber's Gold's owner came in and joined us with a cup of black tea.

'Bill, this is Danny Chang. Danny, this is Bill Brown, Harry's son,' Pat said.

'You're the owner of Amber's Gold right? Must be pretty happy?'

'Yes, and you're the reporter from The Last Newspaper in the World with an interest in the death of our poor, late mayor, Barry Brand, and our racing club?'

I was tempted to say something really Little Texas, like 'you're not from around these parts are you pard'ner?' but decided against it, for now.

'Mr Chang is from Singapore but has interests in our district,' said Pat. He looked around but he need not have worried about anybody overhearing us, as the on-screen commentator was winding up for the next race and the punters filed by after placing their bets. A couple of women wandered by holding wine glasses and wearing tight dresses too light for a winter's day but just right for a day out. They glanced briefly at us. We must have seemed an odd threesome. Me with my unmanageable surfer hair and ill-disciplined tie; Danny Chang with the cowboy hat he was now slowly turning around by the rim; and Pat slouching in a winter tweed coat.

'So you've got an interest in the mayor's death?' I asked.

'Yes, of course, and can I tell you why?'

I nodded but quickly held up my hand, remembering the rark up Harry had given me after the furore following my pic of the dead mayor and my miscommunication with Officer Stead.

'Hold on a minute Mr Chang. Is this on the record or off the record?'

Chang looked at Pat, who shrugged then tilted his head from side-to-side.

'Can we just say that I would rather you didn't use my name at this stage please?'

'On background then,' I said. Harry would maybe smile when he found out I was getting wound into the technicalities of reportage.

'On 'background'. Yes, I like that. Background. Here but not there; there but not here.'

'Of course it reduces the impact of what you might tell me. People might question why you won't put your name to it.'

Leaning forward with his tea cup now mostly emptied, he said: 'But I don't want to make an impact. I just want to help you with your story Bill, if I may call you that.'

It was my turn to shrug. The announcer had started calling the race, so we were pretty much alone in the cafeteria.

'Christine will be here after this race. I will have to go soon.'

'You know that I am part of the group who are interested in developing the Victory Racing Club into a luxury recreational facility?'

Although I knew nothing about this scheme, I thought it would be rude to disagree. I nodded and encouraged him to go on.

'We want to keep the race track and will, in fact, improve on its current status. We can add a golf course and will build an upscale condominium for our visitors and club members. Of course, there is more to it than just the race course.'

Chang was silent then and I put my hands upwards to encourage him to continue.

'We have an option for an interest in the Hot Springs Centre near Victory. They will make an ideal addition to our resort plans.'

I leaned back now. The race was coming to an end. Looking around I could see the jockeys grimly urging on tired horses through the rain as mud flew into view.

'And?' I asked.

'And we are going to transform The Coast Boat Club into a deep-sea fishing jumping off point for high net worth individuals who love to chase tuna and marlin.'

'And...?'

'And what?'

'Mayor Brand. Did somebody kill him because he stood in the way of the grand plan?'

Chang didn't laugh but looked up at the crowd filtering back as the horses returned the birdcage. He looked at Pat then turned his hat around in his hands.

'What you have to realise is these are difficult times to raise money for this kind of venture.'

'Difficult? I'd say impossible.'

'Difficult but not impossible, if you know the right people.'

'Or the wrong people,' Pat said.

'Yes Pat, quite right, the wrong people.'

My phone went. It was Christine wanting to meet up.

'Look, I have to go. What do you mean wrong people?'

Our three heads were by this time quite close together. Chang raised a hand, then dropped it.

'It seems some of our members had their interests taken over by unofficial investors when they couldn't meet certain repayments. These investors seem to have other interests they are putting ahead of our resort plans.'

'Sex, drugs and rock 'n roll by any chance? So why not tell Mr Stead and the local police about all this?'

'We have and they are doing their best, but they don't have the resources for this kind of investigation.'

'So where do I come in, if the combined forces of the police can't solve this case?'

14

TALK TO ME

Where I came in, apparently, is that Chang wanted me to go to Singapore to track down the instigators of all his problems and the alleged murderer or murderers of Mayor Brand. I knew Harry wouldn't bite on such a proposition, as that might have been a little too far out of the office for me to go. We chatted a while, agreed that I'd at least put the idea to Harry. Chang gave me his details and I left to find Christine. We met as she walked back from the stalls. Rain fell hard on the black pavement but Christine was smiling, striding through water in tight leather boots.

'Enjoying yourself are you?' I asked, turning up the hood of my jacket as we hurried over to the car.

She laughed as she pulled open the car door and flung herself in. I chucked my camera gear on to the back seat and climbed in. As she started the car, turned on the wipers and the radio, I looked over at her face. Her hair was slicked back, just like she was a swimmer emerging from a pool. Little droplets of water ran down the side of her face. Her skin was shiny and tight from days in the sun, without having yet become hard from too much exposure to coast life. Opening the glove box, I reached in and found a small pack of tissues. My cold fingers awkwardly pulled over the plastic bag. Taking out a tissue I reached over and wiped water on her left cheek. Driving across the car park towards the gate, she reached up and grabbed the tissue.

'Hey, I can do that, look after yourself,' Christine said, her long fingers folding over mine to extract the tissue. 'You look after yourself. Besides, I've got something to tell you.'

I took a tissue to wipe my own face. The truth is since I had become closer to Angelique, I had become more open and interested in women. When I asked what it was she wanted to tell me, we had a little game of you first.

I told her what Chang had suggested and her response was similar to mine – Harry wouldn't buy it – but she had a different take on Chang's version of events. We were driving around the lakes on our way back to the coast. I'd always found the lakes on a rainy day had a sense of the sinister. Now, as Christine talked, I leaned against the door and looked out the window as choppy little whitecaps licked the lakes and deep mist crept down over bush so water-met-water.

'Bill, you know Chang's got a rep as a player?' Christine said. I looked over at her as she steered the car around a slippery bend, peering intently through the wash of the blades on the windscreen. She suddenly sounded serious.

'I would guess that, being a horse owner. So he likes to gamble. Stands to reason, or is he in too far?'

Christine's voice lightened, she smiled and relaxed as we emerged from a narrow stretch of road to open highway, away from the gloom of the trees. 'That too,' she said, 'but more like a player, player.'

'So he chases the ladies, so...,' I said in what must have been a vaguely mocking tone, because Christine took her eyes off the road and looked over at me. We were now on another narrow stretch of road around a lake. Water lay across the highway but the rain had stopped. Above the range ahead, I could see slices of blue-tinged sky thrown up from coast.

'Hmm, yeah, that too. It's more than that though,' she said.

'You speak from experience?'

'Pretty much. Let's just say I had a lucky escape.'

'Come on babe, you can tell me. I won't tell anyone.'

'Don't 'babe' me. I know what you news guys are like,' she said, suddenly serious.

I tried to back track. 'Sorry. You do know I'm not like that,' I said.

'Not like Harry, you mean? Who took the pic of our mayor lying on his back in a ditch with a hole in his head then?'

'I'm not Harry,' I said, swore and then added: 'You must know that.'

'Did you just swear?'

I apologised and we were quiet for a while as the little car whipped its way up into the hills.

We were silent until the car started to hum down the other side of the range. The plains spread out like a welcome mat to the coast. The rain behind us, the clouds were split with that pale blue sky reflecting a winter sea. Giving an inner sigh, I glanced over at the silent Christine. She was different to Angelique, who flared with annoyance or joy, then freely said what she loved or hated. Christine knew more than I thought a horse-crazy kid could know. Suddenly I admired her joyful resilience, yet was perplexed at how to mine her knowledge without driving her deeper underground.

'Look, I'm sorry,' I said, as she changed to fifth gear and cruised along the straight towards the coast. 'I'm not Harry but this is a very big story for him. Let's not forget we are talking about somebody who has been murdered. Whatever the mayor was up to, and it's looking decidedly dodgy, did he deserve to end up in a ditch with a hole in his head?'

'And have his photo taken by you, then splattered all over our paper?' she neatly added.

'Yeah that too, I suppose.'

We were quiet again then for a while, as she navigated her way through Victory with fruit and vege stalls on one side and a police house, pub and shuttered stores on the other. After we crossed the bridge, we passed a guy riding a large farm horse bare-back. I looked over to see if I could pick out Jimmy Tatua's place and wondered whether his dad was right now cooking up some eel and eggs.

'Okay,' Christine said. 'I don't want this in the paper. This is between you and me. I am just not as heavy-duty as people like you and Harry.'

There she was again comparing me to Harry. Maybe I should really start swearing like the old man. I didn't protest, however, as I wanted to hear what she had to say. The little car was humming along again and we were going quite fast. I reached over and put my hand on her shoulder.

'Look, you don't have to tell me anything. I don't care enough. Hey, I'd rather be out having a surf.'

'Yeah? That's you all over isn't it? Life's a big joke, a bit of dreamtime at the beach,' she said suddenly with a forcefulness that surprised me.

'Nah. Maybe before this I would've, but now...'

Christine took a deep breath as tears ran down her cheeks at a gentle canter.

15

CHRISTINE'S NIGHT OUT

Christine pulled the car over. We were opposite the Hot Pools Centre now, in full weak winter sunshine. It seemed hard to imagine the bucolic country complex being a key component in any upmarket resort plans. As I climbed out of the tiny car I glanced across the plains back to where the deep green of the range seemed to couple with the dark sky. Christine came around and we leaned against the car with our backs to the road, shielding ourselves slightly from the highway. We spoke quietly, even against the noise of passing vehicles.

Christine smiled.

'You know I loved horses when I was growing up. Had the whole pony club thing going on, walls covered in rosettes; and stacks of trophies displayed in prominent positions.'

'Yeah, I can see that. Where'd you live?'

'Up the valley, so it was a big deal to come into town to the club, then later going around the place for competitions.'

'You were pretty good?'

'The folks thought so. You can see a vid of me on YouTube winning the Bay junior eventing champs. Mum did it. It's a hoot.'

I laughed and tried to imagine a younger Christine competing against some of those other pony club kids. It wasn't that hard to picture.

'I can kind of see you doing that but for one flaw – you don't seem at all competitive.'

'Oh I am really, you just don't know it.'

'Sorry, can't see it. I knew some of those pony club kids at school and they could be pretty hard going.'

Christine's face flushed and she looked like she was going to say something to defend her former club mates, but dropped it. Instead, she told me how she also loved writing and sent in reports to the paper.

'The folks raced a couple of horses, just hacks really, so I used to trot along with them to help on race day. One day, we bumped into Harry and got talking. My folks told him how I was at a loose end and mum, pushy as, gave him an ear bashing until he agreed to take me on as a cadet.'

'As a matter of interest, why was Harry there then?'

'The usual reasons, I guess. He was there with Pat McComb. He hasn't much to do with him recently. That's why I think it's a bit odd that he'd send both of us out of town to take a photo of his horse like this.'

'I just thought he wanted to get me out of town for a while or maybe give you some company.'

Christine shook her head. The pony tail was now drier and fluttered in the wind as a logging truck sped past and its wheels almost seemed to crease the road. We were quiet for a minute as the noise faded and the wind subsided.

'You know how you said Harry was at the races with 20 Cents when you met him? Do you know what happened?'

'How do you mean?' she asked, looking up the highway.

I followed her gaze as the truck veered around the next bend.

'Me,' Christine said, gently lowering her head. 'Some of the guys in racing like to party hard. I was pretty young, okay it wasn't long ago, so don't look like that. When I started, mum and dad used to pick me up after going to the races. But they had to go up to Auckland one weekend, so Harry arranged for Mr McComb to take me to the local race meeting.'

She went quiet then. I asked her where, she said, Gatesby, the main city further up the coast. I sometimes went up there for a surf and the nearby beach resort, the Heads, but it reminded me too much of Auckland for me to want to hang around.

'After the races, we were going to drive back home, but Mr

McComb said he wanted to first to go to some party at the Heads,' she was talking quite fast now. 'Said we'd just pop in and show willing to the owners and some other guys. It was an apartment by the beach. You know, in one of those big palaces. I thought it'd be fun,' Christine said, looking over at me as if feeling the need to explain herself. I shrugged.

'It was, at least to start with.'

'How'd old 20 Cents go? I wouldn't have thought he'd had it in him.'

'Yeah, I know what you mean, but he was good, introducing me to everyone. Mr Chang was there and that cop. You know, the one you don't like.'

'Stead?'

'Mmm, that's the one. I was on my own for a while, because Mr McComb was talking with Mr Chang, who was sitting on a couch with two girls. I must have been pretty green then, because it dawned on me that none of the men seemed to be with their wives.'

She was looking straight ahead now. It may have been the late sun breaking through distant clouds but her eyelids were narrowed.

'I wanted to go but Mr McComb laughed and told me to get a drink. There was a bar with lots of booze. I didn't want anything, and just really wanted to get out of there. Stead came over and I felt better. After all he's a cop, right?'

'Right, so what'd he do?'

'Nothing that I know of. We were just chatting. Then one of the girls brought out a pipe and passed it around. When it came to us, I shook my head but Stead said 'it's okay, I won't tell if you don't'. I had a few puffs but I don't know if I inhaled much, as I seemed to cough a lot. Everybody laughed, and I thought it was fun. I was getting tired though and it'd been a hot day. I went out on to the balcony and lay on one of the loungers, watching the surf crash in the evening sun. The noise of the waves seemed deafening from up there. I closed my eyes. I thought I felt somebody's hand between my legs but I couldn't tell you for sure.'

I nodded when she looked at me and didn't say anything.

'Anyway, it was dark when I woke up. It was cold, colder than it should have been for a summer night. I felt pretty bad but I was okay, you know, all in one piece.'

'That's good. Must have felt weird though? Good to get out of there, I suppose.'

'I could hear voices from inside. A man and woman were slumped against the bar arguing, drinks in their hands spilling as they went back and forth. He was a big guy, with a strange, blank face. She was quite tall too but skinny as. I think she was a few years ahead of me at school, quite athletic then.'

I reckoned I knew who they were but didn't say anything.

'Where were the others?'

'Bodies were spread around on sofas or screwed up in big chairs. Guys in their undies and chicks in not much at all. Mostly passed out. I couldn't see Mr McComb and looked over at the couple at the bar. They stopped arguing for a moment and the guy gestured towards a hallway where I could see some closed doors. I went to the first one and opened the door. It was a master bedroom, and Mr Stead and Mr Chang were in this huge bed with a couple of girls going hard at it. You know sometimes how you're shocked and all you can do is stare? That's what happened to me, until Stead lifted his head and roared at me to fuck off. I went to the next room and found Mr McComb lying alone on top of the bed with his pants around his knees, but at least he was on his stomach. I shook him. He opened his eyes and didn't say anything, just looking at me out of the corner of his eyes, blinking. He waved me to get out and said he'd be with me in a moment. I walked out. The couple in the lounge weren't there anymore. I went out of the apartment and stood in the hall. Leaning against the wall, I closed my eyes and started to shake.'

'What happened? Did Pat come out?'

'Yeah, yeah. He'd straightened himself up but his eyes were sliding around all over the place. He told me not to tell Harry. That he'd thought it'd be a bit of fun. I told him I didn't think it was that funny. It was a long drive home that night.'

'Did you say anything to Harry? Is that why he's been so down on Pat?'

'Yeah, I told him. Not everything like I've told you but enough. I love my job and felt embarrassed but thought he should know.'
Christine was quiet then. She shook for a moment. We got back in the car. I drove slowly off.

16

WE LOVE RASTA AND HIPPY BULLSHIT

We went back to the office. I'd already sent the pics, so it was just a matter of retrieving them from the system and tidying them up. Christine went to her desk in the corner to write the copy for what we agreed was just a caption story. The pic of Amber's Gold crossing the line came up pretty well in the end, although it was a bit dark in the winter light. Pat McComb and Chang looked slightly strained instead of triumphant but I'd managed to nudge a smile out of them in one shot. Old Pat's teeth were a bit past it, with gaps here and there. Christine left just as I was checking out the surf report. When I looked up to give her a nod goodbye, I saw that only Harry was left, in his office. I went over but he didn't look up when I entered, so I decided to get right into it or I'd never get out of there for a late surf.

'When were you going to tell me about Christine's big day out with Pat and his friends?' I asked Harry. He pushed his chair back from the desk, stood up and walked over to look out at the window. It was already getting a bit dim out there, so maybe a surf wasn't on after all.

'You didn't need to know. It might've just upset you and put a dampener on today's proceedings.'

'Ya think?' I said, trying to sound sarcastic but really I was more curious about what the old guy was up to. 'Com'n what're you thinking here?'

'Look you might act like young Mr Worldly Wise, Bill, but you're still not as fucked up as the rest of us, yet. If I'd told you what I wanted, and why, you couldn't hide it on your face. It's too open.'

'That's bullshit and you know it.'

Harry came around and sat in one of his chairs opposite me. He shrugged.

'No it's not, and don't talk to me like that. You're still just a reporter here and I'm your editor.'

We both laughed at that, because we both knew that wasn't really the case.

'So...and?'

'Well, I at the very least needed a pic of Pat and Chang together, with that winning look. I wasn't going to push the youngster into doing that, not after what had happened to her before.'

'So what's old Pat up to then? He's just Chang's trainer, isn't he? No big deal, unless you think they're tied up with the mayor's murder.' I said, hoping Harry knew something I didn't and would share it with me.

'Could be. So did you get anything worthwhile out of the pair of them?'

'Chang wants me to go to Singapore to help track down the murderer.'

If he was surprised, Harry didn't show it then.

'I bet he did,' he said. 'What else?'

'He reckons there's another group wanting to get in on this deal they've got going for some kind of country club involving the racing club, the local hot pools, and the fishing club. Sounds a bit suss to me.'

'It's bullshit,' Harry said rather emphatically. 'What'd you make of Christine's story? You know, in the light of Chang's yarn?'

Maybe because I had an eye on the fading light outside, I shook my head to indicate I didn't get it.

'Put it like this: what if Mayor Brand knew something about the plan and the involvement of these guys? Enough to get him killed?' Harry asked.

'That'd make Christine a witness who could put all these guys together.'

We looked at each other. I turned to look at Christine's corner desk where I imagined I saw her light shining.

'Catch you later, I'm going for a surf,' I said, pushing back my chair. Harry went to say something and instead nodded. I watched his back as he returned to his office, peering at his screen. He looked up and, seeing me, waved his hand ushering me out.

I went quickly down the stairs and walked behind The Last Newspaper in the World to where my car was parked. As I drove down the Strand, I heard Rasta music coming out of a takeaway place. In the fading light, a kid was doing some moves in front of no audience I could see. We love Rasta in the Bay, I thought.

It was even gloomier by the time I got to the beach but I could see some beautiful lines stretching out to the horizon. The orange corner streetlight was hissing outside Gordon's place. I parked opposite and got out, sitting on the bonnet to check out the waves. One lone figure sat outside, his board rising and falling through each swell. The waves were almost too high to hold up on the banks of the beach break. The sound of the surf was quite different from that of the constant rumble of an on-shore boil-up. The sea's energy was being delivered in a watery chain, now silent and now thundering. I could never understand when my parents talked about the sound of one hand clapping. Some old hippy bullshit, I used to think, I think. The waves in front of me were like hands folding over, expressing energy; an artist at work on an ozone canvas.

'So, are you going in? It's getting a little dark.'

I turned and saw Angelique standing next to me, her head tilted to one side, the round face quizzical but smiling. She slipped an arm through my mine and held my hand.

'Yes, it is isn't it?'

'I have a gorgeous soup on.'

Looking straight ahead to the sea, I could see the surfer making his way through the white water to shore.

'What sort of soup is it?'

'Onion, of course.'

'Oh.'

'Did I mention we also have rabbit stew?'

'Ah, and Bernie is he, you know?'

'He's eaten; off at the club.' She tugged on my arm. 'I know you don't feel like company but come and share this with me.'

As we got into my car, I glanced over and realised I didn't have my board in the back. I told Angelique and we laughed.

17

THE RABBIT HAS A BREAK

Bernie was in the lounge, checking business news again when we walked in. He looked up and waved. Angelique gestured for me to sit at the dining table. Bernie came out and handed me a beer from the fridge, placing an empty bottle on the bench.

'So how's it going?' he asked.

I knew he wasn't referring to my health.

'Mixed. I think we're on to something but I don't know,' I said, my voice trailing off as I thought of Harry and wondered what he knew or didn't know and if he knew what he knew, why didn't he just tell me. 'Have you heard anything from the cops?'

'No, I must say the drums have gone very quiet,' Bernie said, adding, 'that does sometimes mean they are up to something but want to keep it low key.'

'Or they know not much more than we do, or even less?'

'No I don't think so, but you know the saying 'Coastlands cops, they never get their man'.'

'That's a bit brutal isn't it, Bernie?'

We laughed a bit. Angelique put down a bowl of onion soup. Steam rose between Bernie and I.

'Yes that may be son but you ask Harry, he knows more than I do. Well, must be off to the club; it's darts night.'

I started to sip at the soup as he went out the door holding a set of darts in one hand. The soup tasted better than I thought it'd be.

'So my soup is not horrible then?'

'Hmm, yeah good,' I said as I slurped down another spoonful. 'What is it?'

'*Soupe à l'oignon gratinée* but please don't make that noise.'

Looking up, I saw her black eyebrows raised and a slight tilt of her head. It wasn't the first time she'd queried my eating habits. I'd seen her occasionally wince across the café as I chomped down on a defenceless pie. Harry and I had lower standards in dinner time etiquette; in fact I think the old boy was worse than me, if that was possible. I wondered why Angelique liked me if she hated my eating habits so much.

Angelique bent over and wiped a tiny piece of onion off my bottom lip and kissed me. The rabbit was left to its own devices for a while.

Angelique's room was a bit cold. It was fully dark now and she was asleep. We were heavily covered in blankets and a duvet and lay close together in the double-bed. I could feel in my left arm the heat from her body, so alive but so relaxed. I reached over and ran the back of my hand down her side from the bottom of her ribs to her hip. Even in the dark, I could see her lips in silhouette parting, her eyebrows frown. She reached over with her right hand to touch my face, and then rolled over on her side away from me. A message came through on my phone. I reached down and pulled it out of my jacket. It was Harry: 'Breakfast. 0800 @ Gordon's.' I okayed him back and thought briefly about why he wanted to meet at Gordon's for breakfast but this quickly gave way to a vision of the lines that night coming into the beach. If I woke early enough, I could get a surf in before the meeting. I reached over and kissed Angelique on the back of her neck and went to sleep.

The waves the next morning were good. Not quite as large as the night before, which in some ways was a bit disappointing, but it did at least let me get out quicker for each ride. I told Angelique about Harry's text and she was quite surprised.

'Gordon does not usually open the café for breakfast in the winter,' she said, pulling a perfect turtle-neck sweater on, and then rubbing her hands together against the cold. 'Maybe Harry has called him to alert him to this possibility?'

'Quite likely, I think, always with the planning, Harry,' I said from the bed. I remembered my board wasn't in the back of the car.

'So you are not going out this morning?'

'No, I haven't got time to go back to town and get my board.'

'Oh, why do you not use Bernie's. I am sure he will not worry.'

'I'm not that keen. I've seen the old boy's dunga.'

'Dunga?'

'You know, big and heavy. Not overly responsive.'

Angelique laughed and leant over me, taking hold my shoulders with her small hands.

'So choosey. I think you are a little tired and scared of the cold water.'

She went out of the room and I could hear her waking up Bernie to tell him I was going to borrow his board. He said something back to her but I couldn't hear what he said, although it sounded like assent.

Angelique came back into the room, her black hair swinging and her eyes alive. 'Yes, you may use his board but you must take special care. You must go now, because I have to go and help Gordon set up for the day.'

I called out thanks to Bernie as I went down the hallway and he reminded me to look after his beloved – I think he meant his board. Angelique took me out to the garage and opened it up before walking off to the café. In the half light, I could see the long board slung on a rack along the wall of the garage. I'd forgotten it was a pintail, narrowing tightly as the shape ran down from the full nose to the tail. I had to admit: it wasn't a bad looking board. Picking it up off the rack, it was heavy but it was beautifully balanced as I carried it out. I got my gear out of the car and changed in the garage. It was a bit nippy but the wet suit helped. As I walked past the house towards the beach, Bernie appeared on the door step in flannel pyjamas and gave me the thumbs up.

'I'll look after her,' I called out. Bernie waved and went inside.

Looking down the beach, I could see the day was going to be clear as a slow blue light crept up from the horizon. The swell was smaller but the occasional big one swept through, cracking out ozone into the early morning air. Sitting out the back on the big board, I felt awkward but not too cold. Although I was in a hurry, kind of, I waited and felt the lift of the board up and over the swell rolling through. I felt more fish than bird; there was no flying on Bernie's board, just feeling of being more fully connected to the water. I paddled further out than I normally would, just to give the longer board more room to drop into the wave than on my short board. As I rose over a swell I could see the horizon feathering, indicating a good set wave on the way. Turning, I felt the adrenalin surge mixed with the fear of the unknown. Then, as the wave self-inflated, grew higher, approached faster and started to lift through me, I paddled into that other world, where there is only light and sound. The pintail did its work, its tight tail helping me drop down to the bottom of the wave and quickly turn the board to snake up and across the face. Water like the strongest, coldest shower flowed over my back, but I crouched forward and pushed through out on to the face. Normally, I would kick out of the wave as the wall stood up and prepared to crumble but the big board was slower than I was used to, and at the last minute I twisted around to face the beach, crouching to take the impact as the board dropped down through the foam. The boom from the collapsing wave felt like a jet had landed on the beach but I hung on and managed to catch a small reform wave, only to fall over as I stood up. I had just emerged from below the water, grabbed the board and prepared to paddle back out when I saw Bernie standing on the sand dunes waving.

'Nice wave. Nine out of 10 for the dismount though,' he said when I reached him. He held up his watch. 'Harry rang. He wants you down at the café, now.'

I unzipped and rolled down the top of the wet suit.

Bernie handed me a towel.

'So you and Angelique,' was all he said as we walked across the road.

I looked over and waited for the wisdom I was sure was coming, but it didn't and we walked in silence down to the garage. We discussed the possibility of a shower but I just ran some warm water over my head and tried to shake the tangles out of my hair. Bernie leaned in the doorway and pulled a face, saying 'you really should try harder, for Harry's sake.'

I shrugged and gently closed the door to get changed.

'You know he's greatly depending on you now,' Bernie called

through the door.

I wanted to pull a Harry and tell him to 'f off', but I succumbed and asked Bernie why.

No reply came back, and when I came out Bernie was in the kitchen pouring a coffee. He held up his cup in a goodbye salute, his head to one side.

'Thanks for lending me the board, it's cool,' I said as I waved at him and got out quickly.

18

HARRY GETS SERIOUS

I felt great as I walked up the path to the café, ready for the day ahead. Is this how the jockey felt when he crossed the line on Amber's Gold? Was he smiling at me or just, smiling? Was this how Diana feels when she meets one of Harry's editorial deadlines and files a story? Is that why she is so into it and rather derisory of my efforts? Would I ever be into it in the same way? As I arrived at the café, I looked again at Diana, and how intensely she was focusing on what was being said. I couldn't hear as I stood at the café door looking in. She wasn't rapt as such, more focused – more, into it, like I was as the swell lifted me for a wave.

'Shot Bill,' Neil said quietly to me as I squeezed in between him and Diana.

Angelique was leaning over pouring Harry a coffee. They looked up at me and said something I didn't quite catch. She squeezed his shoulder and they both laughed, Harry shaking his head as he took a sip. Angelique came and stood behind me, close to my back.

'Bonjour, what does monsieur want for breakfast?' she said, pressing her stomach into my back.

I looked around, Neil was studiously stirring his coffee; Diana was looking straight at me, every hair in place, make up perfect.

Harry had decided we should have this breakfast meeting to discuss where we were going with the Brand murder story. This was a first, and a bit of a surprise, as he wasn't at his best at breakfast. I knew. Often I would come in from a dawnie surf feeling like I'd been re-made as a person, chilled. Harry would be sitting at the kitchen table, dressed for a day at The Last Newspaper in the World but loitering over a large coffee. He'd look at me and, just when I thought he'd frown or make a smart arse remark, he often just slightly smiled and jerked his head slightly up. This morning we were at Gordon's and he was all business.

Angelique was right, Gordon didn't usually open for breakfast in the winter, so the 'Closed' sign remained on the café door. Two elderly ladies, looking remarkably healthy in their track suits, jackets and beanies, knocked on the door. Harry waved, I thought, rather imperiously for them to go away but one I recognised as Mrs Ferguson, a teacher who had helped me through a bad patch at school. She was tall for an old chick and her red hair was tucked under her hat, although a couple of greying streaks fell loosely down her neck. She waved at me when I turned and I looked at Harry, who rolled his eyes in the direction of the door. He may have been regretting his decision for a breakfast meeting. I went over and unsnibbed the locked door.

'Hello there William is Gordon open for breakfasts now?' she asked.

'No Mrs Fergusson, sorry, we are just having a meeting here this morning.'

'That Gordon, he could at least put up a 'Private Function' notice.'

I didn't think Gordon ran to private function notices but smiled and told her I'd pass the message on.

'So William, how are you going working with Harry on The Last Newspaper in the World? It must be exciting for you? Why are you meeting here?'

I wondered that myself and look around to see Harry signalling me to hurry up. Agreeing with Mrs Ferguson that I'd talk to her students about a career in journalism, I closed and locked the door. As I walked back to the table, where Angelique was placing my breakfast, I wondered how I could tell anybody about this work. I'm in a career? I asked myself. I looked at the others around the table with Harry. Glen, Neil and Diana – each one applied themselves more greatly than I ever could. Even as I sat down, I was vaguely mournful as my seat faced away from the window. I could not see the morning sun running across the sea to light up the dunes over the road.

I hadn't ordered but Angelique had made me my favourite, La Forestière, a crêpe with mushrooms in a sauce, with an extra of bacon. Diana leaned over towards me. I could smell her perfume as it battled with the aroma of the mushrooms breaking free as I cut through the thin package.

'Special treatment for William then,' she said not so quietly as the others couldn't hear. They all laughed, apart from Harry who just frowned.

'Enough of this you lot,' he said. 'I want us to get more of a grip on this story. We have been ahead in spite of the police ban on us but we are now in danger of falling behind even with the police ban lifted. Glen can you give us an update on what's happening with the strands of this story?'

About this time I glanced at the wall behind Glen's head. He was starting his round up of events so far when I looked at a picture Gordon had screwed on to the wall. The scene was one of those ones where a stormy sea breaks on boulders. The picture sat like a prisoner in a frame behind glass. The storm was silent and the waves were frozen in anger. As I looked at the picture, I saw two figures walking across the boulders into the sea. I realised the glass was reflecting Mrs Fergusson and her friend standing across the road, looking back at the café. I could see the dunes across the road and a touch of cool, calm sea, the clear winter sky was sharper relief. The two women started walking and for a moment I wondered if they were going to pass through my reflected beach to the stormy scene of the picture.

'Bill, are you with us? What do you think of what Glen said about Brand?' Harry said, clicking his fingers as if to wake me up. 'We don't really know enough about him, do we? You know, what sort of person he was? has he got any enemies? that sort of thing.'

'Ah, Harry,' Neil said before I could say anything. 'I do think there was more to him than we know.' He looked at me and I nodded so as to encourage Neil further. 'Well, from what I can tell Mr Brand seems to have been very much a full time mayor. However, records show he was a director, or shareholder, in a number of companies.'

Harry leaned forward.

'What sort of companies?' he asked.

Neil, who before this had been drawing a cartoon I couldn't quite make out on a napkin, pulled a sheaf of papers out of his shoulder bag.

'There are things like the Brand Pastoral Farming Limited and other companies that look like family holdings.'

Just as Harry was going to open his mouth, Glen interjected:

'That's to be expected, Harry. Putting the family farming interests into companies helps separate out his interests from those of the council. There is more though. Go on Neil.'

It occurred to me then that Glen had been helping Neil. Maybe I should try it some time.

'In the past year, Mr Brand and interests associated with him have been involved in some new companies,' Neil said.

'Again, what sort of companies are these – fig farms or hedgehog harvesting?' Harry said, a little sharply but he couldn't help himself.

Neil shuffled his papers, pushing the documents relating to farming interests below a new set.

'Now these are quite different. They seem more likely to be involved in property of some sort or tourism businesses. At least that's what I can tell from the titles.'

'What's in a name?' Harry said and glumly passed a hand over the remaining spikes on his head. 'Come on Neil, what more have you got? We can't do much with this lot.'

'Harry, take it easy,' Glen said, holding up a hand. Neil took a sip of his coffee, and I heard Diana taking a breath beside me. 'Look, he's dug out some interesting stuff right?'

'Maybe, but anybody could get it.'

'Well they haven't and I'd like to see if we can take it further,' Glen said.

'Fine. Anything else?' Harry asked Neil.

'Not too much, but one of the properties is that place where Bill's friend works.'

I looked sideways at him and then quickly over to Harry. 'Which friend?' we both asked at the same time.

'You know, that woman with the big car who works at the Captain's Table.'

Emily, I thought. Harry and I looked at each other, his hair seeming to bristle.

'So our dead mayor just happens to own a property,' said Glen, quickly. 'Does it really mean anything?'

'Yeah, of course,' Harry said, reluctantly I thought. 'Still, not just any property is it?'

'Sure, but I think we have to be careful about making too much out of this stuff,' Glen said.

'True but sometimes a bit of a beat up will get things running.'

'Come on Harry, the guy's dead. I think we have to be a bit sensitive how we handle it,' Glen said, just quickly looking around Neil, Diana and me.

Harry was quiet for a moment. 'Sensitive. Like did the mayor have a policy on ethical investments and so on?'

'You might not like it but brothels are legal in our part of the world, if the council approves,' Glen said.

'How very twenty first century,' Harry said, a little grumpily I thought.

Glen ignored him but told Neil to go through some of the other names involved in any of the companies and properties.

'Brand's funeral is today,' Diana interjected into the momentary silence, 'and Stead has told me we should be there to take some pics.'

'We'll be there,' Harry said bluffly. 'I don't need that feller telling me what to do.'

'What pics in particular?' Glen asked.

'Well that's the thing. He was pretty specific, saying to get pics of the group but also a guy who might seem out of place. Just said we'd know him when we see him. He might be close to the family but out of place.'

'Is that it?' Harry said, swore under his breath. 'Stead tells a good story.'

'Harry, it might be worth something,' Glen said.

'Okay, Diana you go to the funeral. Bill I want you to take the pics.'

I just heard that last bit, because I was handing my empty plate up to Angelique.

'Me?' I said, and I couldn't believe how squeaky my voice sounded. 'Ah, me? Diana's going, so can't she take the pics too?'

Harry looked at me hard. 'Nah you take the pics. Okay, let's get back to the office. Pay on your way out. Glen can you take my car back? I'll go back with Bill.'

Generous as ever, I thought, invite us all out for breakfast then make us pay. As the others filed up to pay Gordon, Harry asked Angelique for a couple more coffees. I glanced up at the picture on the wall. Movement in the sun had obscured the view of the beach. The storm was once again frozen in two-dimensions and I could just see a reflection of Diana's blonde hair light up as she stepped outside.

The coffee came for Harry and me, then Angelique joined us with her own cup. 'This is a bit confusing,' I thought, as Harry slowly stirred his coffee but didn't drink from it. Angelique looked at me and smiled. Gordon walked past our table to click open the café door.

'So how was the surf?' Harry asked. I knew then this was going to be personal. Dad was usually so direct, only edging around the personal stuff.

'Good. Look, what's this about? I've got a funeral to go to, remember.'

Angelique lifted her fingers off the table. I loved how expressive they were in their smallness.

'Okay, where are you going with all of this?' Harry said, raising his hands out wide.

'Let's not have this conversation now, dad. You're too busy.'

19

GOODBYE MR BRAND, HELLO MRS BRAND

Later that day I found myself driving over to the town's sports centre. It was the biggest venue in the place, so was better able to cater for the crowd expected for the mayor's funeral service. Diana was with me. She was dressed in black, tight but conservative with a jacket to match. Her blonde hair touched the top of the jacket perfectly and she looked poised even sitting in the passenger seat of the work car. I kept on inventing excuses to look over her way as we drove, looking out for a stream of cars that wasn't there coming to a side road. Then she turned to me.

'So what did he want?'

I looked around. She was looking directly at me. Although I didn't want to answer the question, I was grateful for the opportunity to check out her beauty face on, close up. I looked ahead and took the corner into the driveway leading into the sport centre.

'The usual, you know, where am I going with the story? what am I doing with my life? some personal stuff. You know the kind of thing old folks ask kids.'

I glanced quickly over to Diana and she just slightly tipped her head so the blonde hair caressed her right shoulder.

'Not really. You're not a kid. What do you mean?'

Of course, her direction and her life had probably never been questioned. Then I remembered Stead's attack on her, her strength and how she remained poised. Reflected in her blue eyes, my lack of commitment seemed weak, even shambling.

'Let's talk about this later. We've got a job to do now, haven't we?' I said, taking a stab at conviction. It was pretty much what I had said to Harry anyway, but probably a bit more gently than I'd cut down the old man's attempt to piece my life together.

She reached over and put a perfect hand on the shoulder of my jacket, saying 'I'm not letting you off that easily. We'll talk later. Or will Angelique object?'

'Of course not,' I said, a little too hastily. Angelique probably would object, although not in the way somebody like Diana might. 'Come on, we know what we've got to do here, right?'

We parked the car. I was nervous as I'd never covered a funeral before, although I'd been to one or two. Stead, having told Diana we should attend and look for somebody who stood out, was standing by the door with a couple of colleagues. I went to walk in but noticed Diana was looking through her purse.

'You alright?' I asked.

She looked up with a smile like a sunrise shining up from a morning sea.

'Fine. Ready to go.'

We walked through the door, nodding at Stead and his team as we went by. He didn't say anything but just kept on talking. In their suits and sunnies they looked like pretty tough guys. Inside, the hall was buzzing, but not with excitement. It was the low sort of sound like an amplified expression of concern. We sat at the back. Diana leaned over and told me I was going to have to go up front to take pics. I nodded and stayed where I was for the time being.

Mayor Brand certainly seemed to have been a great guy. Well, that's what everybody who spoke reckoned. Seemed he was quite the old rocker too. His Harley was mounted on the stage next to his coffin, an old Credence Clearwater number rumbled out through the sports centre's faulty sound system. I caught some of the words as I walked down a side aisle to get closer to the front. From what I could hear *'Lookin' out my Backdoor'* seemed quite a happy song but some of the words were a bit strange for the mayor. *'Tambourines and elephants are playin' in the band. Won't you take a ride on the flyin' spoon'.* What was all that about? Maybe it was just a song, like maybe he was just a small town mayor.

The place was full and when I reached the front I took a couple of wide shots of the crowd. Some in the crowd looked a bit annoyed at me taking pics and when I added a long lens to the camera and started taking shots of the front row, a security officer came over and yanked my sleeve to clear me out. Stead was standing by the doorway. He adjusted his glasses as I went by and smiled. Or was that a smirk?

I walked across the driveway and stood at the front row of parked cars. Slouching against a car, I looked at the pics on the camera. Inside the hall, I could hear sounds from the service. Noise of a combined song mumbled along, more speeches. Then silence. This must be it, I thought, and raised the camera to fix the lens on the doorway. I looked upwards and saw the increasing cloud cover borrow some light from winter's weak sunshine. The car I was leaning on was a farm ute, so I went around the back, jumped on and took up position leaning across the cab.

Diana came out first, striding towards me looking serious in her black dress. She stopped and stood right there on the steps looking at me and mouthing something. I waved for her to get out of the way before the pall-bearers came out on to the steps carrying the coffin. They stopped briefly, before going down the steps to the back of the hearse. Behind them came the family and close friends. I was in business but taking pics of this group was tricky with the undertakers and pallbearers standing around the back of the car.

Jumping down from the ute and quickly moving closer, I crouched down to get a shot of the family. Mrs Brand, even dressed down appropriately for the occasion, was stunning. Tall, thin, and olive skinned, her light brown hair fell over her face as she looked down from the stairs through the screen of large dark glasses. Her lips were full and through the lens I could see they were coloured with what looked like an iridescent pink lipstick. I held her in my lens and followed her as she leaned over to her left to talk to a guy at the end of the row. I saw she was pointing at me and took a closer look at the tall man in a suit and heavy dark glasses. Suddenly his picture blurred slightly and I realised he was striding towards me. Standing behind him I could see Pat McComb and Michael Chang talking and looking our way. Hauling the camera quickly up, I took a shot of the guy advancing on me. In my lens it registered he seemed like a larger version of Mayor Brand. I didn't have time to digest these thoughts as he was approaching quickly, so I held on to Diana's upper arm and pulled her with me towards our car.

'Hey, what are you doing?' she said and started to pull away. I let her go and walked on as if nothing had happened.

'Come on let's get back to the office. Now,' I said as she caught up.

Behind me I could hear steps becoming increasingly loud.

Diana tried to keep up with me, which she did surprisingly easily given her dress and heels. When we reached the car, we jumped in and I immediately locked the doors.

'A bit dramatic,' said Diana, pulling down the visor glancing into the mirror.

I was chucking my gear in the back when I saw our pursuer come to a halt next to her passenger side door and start knocking on the window. Diana jumped and I started the car, backing out as the suit continued banging on her window. At about this point I wished the company cars were a bit gutsier, but Diana called for me to slow down.

'Maybe he just wants to talk to you. We haven't even got our seat belts on. Stop right now.'

I gunned it out of the sports centre driveway and stopped when we reached the road. In the rear view mirror I could see the guy standing in the drive looking at me. He was joined first by Chang, then Pat and Stead.

'What was all that about?' Diana asked. She laughed and punched me on the shoulder lightly.

'I think I just pissed somebody off,' I said, looking unnecessarily in the rear vision mirror. Nobody was following us, but it was that kind of a day.

'You know, you have a talent for doing that don't you?'

'No, not really, but who was that guy chasing us?'

'You, Bill, chasing you.'

'Thanks for your support. What would you've done if he'd got hold of me?'

'Turn left.'

We were approaching a roundabout into town. Diana was looking straight ahead, but she quickly glanced over at me with a smile.

Taking the turn too wide, I asked her again about the chaser. Diana agreed he looked like the dead mayor, so maybe he was a brother or another close relative. But her attention turned to Brand's widow.

'Stunning looking isn't she, even in grief?'

'Even in grief.'

'Did you see the dress she was wearing? That's a lot of money right there.'

'So where do you think the brother, or whatever he is, fits in?' I asked.

'Why don't you ask him?'

'No, why don't you?'

'Me?' Diana said, shaking her head and laughing. I looked too closely as her blonde hair scuffed the back of her neck. She yelled at me to watch where I was going as I narrowly avoided a kid crossing the road on his skateboard. He gave me the finger and I recognised him from school, although he was younger.

'Kids today – look at that behaviour.'

'Just watch where you're going,' Diana said.

'I do think the family guy might respond better to you than me, particularly as he seems to object to having his pic taken.'

Diana was silent. She pulled down the sun shade and quickly looked in the mirror.

'Let's ask Harry,' she replied.

Dad was in his office when we returned. Diana went over to her desk and tidied something up. I saw her looking at the glass on her phone. What was she looking at? I downloaded the pics and added them to the access file. Opening the last pic, I saw it was a bit out of focus but thought it might still be useable. Walking over to Diana's desk, I saw she was on her Facebook page.

'Let's go and see Harry.'

'Sure. I'm just letting my friends know about your drama. Do you do it on purpose?'

I shook my head and started walking over to Harry's office. He looked up as I entered. Diana came in just as I was closing the door.

'Sorry,' I said.

'That's a bit rude.'

'Okay, so you had a bit of fun at the funeral,' Harry said, leaning back in his chair. 'Tell me about it.'

20

BRANDSVILLE IN THE RAIN

Harry's solution was to send us both out to the street where the Brand family lived. He'd listened to Diana's version of events at the funeral service, including my reaction to the pursuit across the sports centre car park. He looked at me with pursed lips and eyebrows deepening. Running a hand over his prickly head, he suggested it would have been a much better story if I'd stayed put and been overhauled by my pursuer.

'Really? Besides, that's an expensive camera we're using,' I said.

'Yeah, we wouldn't want to get the camera damaged,' Harry said, the tapped his fingers on his desk top.

'Okay, this is what I want you to do,' he said, looking at us.

'Both of us?' asked Diana, quite quickly as she frowned and looked at me.

'Yes, do you think you can manage it?'

We both nodded. As I looked at Diana, I was beginning to, if not understand, at least realise the drive she had for the job.

'This afternoon, see what you can find out about the family – Mrs Brand and the brother, particularly. See if we can find some link to land deals or that other business at the race course. Go out to where they lived and get a feel for their relationships.'

'Oh I don't know about that. Do you think people will want to talk to us about this sort of thing?' Diana said, looking first at Harry and then at me, as if to ask for support.

'Look, Brand might be our town's favourite son...'

'Or might not be,' I interjected. Harry gave me a swift 'shut up' look through his narrowed eyes.

'...but there will be some nosy neighbours out there who know something useful. So get out there and find out more than we know now.'

'How do you know what the neighbours know will in any way be useful?' I asked, and heard a quiet sigh from Diana.

'Guarantee it,' Harry said.

When we hesitated in our seats, Harry waved us away with a final 'now'.

On our way back to our desks we stopped to talk to Glen, telling him of Harry's plan.

'Makes sense,' he said. 'What I suggest you do is search in the files and online for anything on the two of them. Diana, why don't you look out for info about Mrs Brand; Bill, you can take his brother.'

We didn't answer and he asked us if we were okay. For once Diana's perfect poise looked a bit ruffled, her face reddened. 'Play nicely,' Neil said.

Compared to his brother, Steve Brand was practically Mr Invisible. Whereas Mayor Barry Brand was all over the place, opening this, closing that, and commenting on everything from helping business start-ups in the town to the growing drug problem, Brother Brand was much more under the radar. A search of official records at the Companies Office showed him to be a director of Coastlands Property Management and a couple of other companies.

Neil came in the office carrying a file of papers and sat at his desk. I went over to say 'hi' to him and asked if I could look through those land documents he'd had earlier. His desk was a mountain of paper but he quickly found what I was wanting.

'What do you want these for?' he asked.

'Well, we're just having a look at the mayor's brother, Steve. Do you know any more about him?'

'Not really. He's been around but mostly in the shadow of Barry, who's been more out there. Look through those land records if you like. I can't remember if he shows up. Let me know if you need me to search for anything.'

Glancing at his desk, I saw a cartoon of Harry's office. Diana and I were standing on either side of his desk, and he was saying something to us I couldn't quite read. Neil slid his hand over the paper, making it disappear somehow.

As we drove out, Diana told me what we should do. Technically, of course, we discussed it. It was later in the day, around dinner time. Ideal apparently for door stopping, Diana said. I was feeling a bit peckish but I could see the sense.

'Have you ever done much door stopping before?' I asked her.

'Not really but we did a module at school. So it's pretty straight forward, even for somebody like you. We're going out to talk to the neighbours but don't get dragged off into all sorts of side stories.'

'The interesting stuff then.'

'No, certainly not, just concentrate on what we are there for rather than being diverted away.'

'But how will you know what's important and what's not?'

'Look, do you really want to do this or shall I do it on my own,' she said, as we approached the area.

'Well, there is a good surf running. Do you think you could manage?'

Diana ignored me and pulled into Brand Place. I asked her if she thought it was a bit weird, the mayor living in a street carrying his family name

'The Brands were big around here, so I suppose they got naming rights on the streets. You know they created this suburb, Brandsville. I have been doing some research on my own, not just bumming info off Neil.'

'That's a bit unfair,' I said half-heartedly.

We got out of the car. It was already dark and clouds were driving lower to deliver showers. Brand Place was a cul-de-sac, a dead end street lined with what in summer would be quite pretty trees. The sections laid out in the open style with few fences and front yards running right down to the road. We knew the Brands lived right at the end of the street, so we started at the top and worked our way down to the end, me on the right and Diana on the left. She was correct about it being a good time to call in that most people were home around dinner time. What they may not have covered on the module at school was that, for some reason, some people don't liked being disturbed when trying to digest a winter-time meal. The man who answered the door at the first house had the appearance of what I imagined to be a professor. Cardigan, thinning hair and squinting through glasses, he looked at me quizzically as I tried to explain what we were doing there.

'So you're here to dig up the dirt on our mayor and his poor family?'

'No, no, no, we just want to get more background on his life and times for a tribute to him.'

'Who is it, dear?' a woman came up behind the prof. She was much younger than the man, long black hair falling over a pullover. Tight jeans only accentuated her trimness and heavy glasses highlighted the interest of her eyes.

'Some guy from The Last Newspaper in the World. Wants to dig up some dirt on the mayor and his family.'

'No, no that's not right,' I protested but he had already shut the door.

The next couple of houses had drawn pretty much the same result, so I was getting a bit desperate by the time I got down to the last three on my side of the cul-de-sac. Looking across the road, I could make out Diana standing in the light of a doorway, chatting away to an elderly couple. Peals of laughter waved at me and I could see her hair flash as she rocked her head back. I knocked on the next door and it was immediately opened by a middle-aged guy in a black singlet, shorts and fluffy socks. The house was brick, flat and ran a long way back on the section. I could see down a hallway into a lounge where a big screen television dominated, so giant rugby players seemingly screamed out of the wall. He thrust his head out around the doorway and jutted it upwards in the direction of Diana and her new best friends.

'What's going on over there? A party or something?'

'Yeah, looks like it. Nah, we're just chatting to people about the tragic death of Mr Brand. I'm from the paper.'

'Our one?' I nodded and hoped, and then he asked me what I wanted to know. I wasn't quite ready for that.

'Oh, how's the rugby going? Who's winning?'

'Nobody. It's pretty tight.'

I thought he was going to close the door, and invoked a good Harry swearing in my head.

'This won't take long. We just want to paint a bit of a picture of the Brands, you know, happy families and all that.'

'Happy families? You are joking aren't you?'

'She's all cool there, right?' I offered.

'She's cool alright,' he said, rubbing the bristles greying across his cheeks. 'Nah make that hot, she's real hot.'

'You are talking about the family, right?'

'Mrs Brand, yeah, she's pretty hot.'

'And the family? How'd they get on?'

'Hot and cold, I'd say.'

Wanting to break out of the code words, I decided it was time to plunge in, hot or cold.

'So it wasn't all happy families at the Brands then?'

'Far from it, at least recently, I'd say,' he said and looked over his shoulder towards the lounge.

'What do you mean?'

'The police were called a couple of times. I don't know if he hit her or not but she wouldn't come out of the house for a couple of days afterwards. Cars coming and going. That sort of thing. Have you seen their place yet? Hard to know what goes on in there.'

I was scribbling away and trying to order my thoughts at the same time. Nobody had mentioned any incidents involving the police at the Brand house. Located at the end of the street it was surrounded by high concrete walls, like a compound, with gates across the front.

'Police? Don't think I'd heard anything about that,' I said, taking the risk of putting my ignorance out there. The guy didn't seem worried.

'Why would you?' he said and shrugged. I heard a roar from inside. 'I better go, it looks like it might be getting interesting,' he said. I took his name and contact number, swearing not to use his details.

The door wasn't answered at the next house even though the lights were on and I could hear the game in the background.

One household to go and I could see Diana still had two to work through. The last house before the Brands' was wedged on a triangular section between the previous one and the walled property beside it. It was probably no less in size but seemed dwarfed by the scale of additions to the multiple stories of the mayor's house. The concreted wall hung like a giant wave waiting to crash on the street around it. I walked down the footpath, passing a tidy garden. A lone lemon tree sat in the middle of a neat lawn. A ginger was cat curled on a well-swept and clean front porch. The presentation suggested pride in their world.

The door was answered by an elderly man, sort of plump in the way of more mature guys but I guessed he had probably been short and round for much of his life. His wife came down the hallway behind him, wearing heavy glasses and touching the wall with one hand. I introduced myself and, in the spirit of Diana, tried to make a joke, it didn't work but the old girl invited me in for a cup of tea.

Stan and Eileen had lived in Brand Place since it was formed 20 years ago when the suburb was developed by the mayor's father.

'Good bloke he was. Not like his son,' Stan said as we walked into the kitchen. 'This is bit of a mistake. It could take hours, so I hope you're not in hurry,' Stan said, nodding towards Eileen as she worked her way to the kettle, filled it with water and plugged it in.

'Not bad for a blind old girl, are you honey?' Stan called out to his wife, adding quietly to me. 'I've got to let her do these things or she gets cranky with me.'

'I can hear that you know,' Eileen said, looking in our direction. She waved a hand lightly in a cupboard and found some biscuits.

'She's got much better hearing that I have,' Stan said.

'Yes and I'm not as blind as you either,' she said.

Stan shook his head at me.

I was wondering where this was going to go, thinking of the time.

'Did you hear much from your neighbours?' I tried.

'Lots of cars coming and going at all hours,' Stan said.

'I don't think the young man was talking about cars, Stan,' Eileen said. 'You know, we live next to them but hardly ever speak to them. Of course, Mr Brand was there for years but she's new. I sometimes wonder why they got married. They do, I mean did, seem to talk a lot in loud voices.'

'Even I could hear them and I'm the deaf one,' Stan said.

'It's not about you Stan. It was worse recently, she would start off at him and he would try to keep his voice low. You could tell he was struggling, because the more she said, the louder he got, until they were both at it. Eventually she would go quiet and he'd have the final say.'

'I reckon he was a proper bastard, I don't care how you media guys write him up,' Stan said.

'You said the noise, arguments were worse recently. Anything different around the place?' I said, thinking 'please give me something'.

Stan tapped his fingers on the table, while Eileen sat and started to pour the tea. Holding on to the cups, she was able to guide the stream in without a miss and feel the hot measure as it neared the top.

'Are you going to tell him?' she said to Stan.

'Yes, but it might be nothing,' he said.

'Don't worry Stan, this is between you and me, no names and all that,' I said.

Stan shrugged. 'Things seem to have been worse since his brother has been on the scene.'

'Oh, why's that?' I said, trying to casually take up one of the biscuits Eileen offered.

'You know the mayor was out of town for that trip to China a couple of weeks ago? So Gerry, that's his brother, seemed to be around a lot during that time. It was only a week, so I thought he was just around looking after things or doing something. But then

Eileen said one morning she hadn't heard his car leaving, so he must've been there all night.'

'He wouldn't know,' Eileen said, gesturing at Stan with a crumbled biscuit of her own. 'Sleeps like a log, snoring his jolly head off all night long.'

'Maybe Gerry just stayed late, had a few drinks and didn't want to drive home,' I said.

'Maybe, but there weren't any raised voices but lots of laughing during the time the mayor was away,' Stan said. 'Isn't that right, Eileen?'

'And other noises too,' she said. Her tiny face was pinched into a tight smile as she leaned forward. 'I said to Stan 'Stan, I think those two are up to no good'.'

'So what do you think?' Stan asked me.

'Well guys, very interesting,' I said. I slurped my tea as I thought it was more than very interesting, more like 'bloody interesting' as Harry would say.

'Then there was that Stead, wasn't there Stan?' Eileen said. She raised one thin arm and waved tiny, creased fingers at her husband.

'Yes, yes. Eileen didn't see him but I saw him coming and going, like the big man in his police car.'

'How'd you know Stead?'

'Oh he used to go to school with our Tommy. Hope you don't mind dear, but he was a total prick.'

'I didn't know Stead was from around here?'

'He's not, we sent Tommy away to finish school in Auckland. Didn't want our Tommy roughing it with the others at Coast High did we Eileen.'

'He's a nice boy our Tommy.'

The front door bell rang an old time 'ping, pong'.

'I think I know who that is. I'd better be going. Thanks a lot of the tea and bikkie.'

Stan walked me down the hall, while Eileen cleared away the dishes. I heard one or two fall into the sink, but nothing broken.

As we reached the door, Stan gently held my elbow. 'Now remember, Bill, please don't use our names. We don't need the trouble.'

'Sure, sure, it's what we call 'on background',' I didn't know if it was called that but I had seen it somewhere in a movie.

'Good man, good man,' Stan said, and we shook hands.

Diana was standing on the path looking up at the porch. The rain was coming down now and sweeping through her hair as it picked up the porch lights. She didn't look very impressed. The collar of her snug red coat was pulled up around her neck, and I tugged my jacket hoodie over my head. We walked shoulder to shoulder up the street; as though our combined effort could pinch open a narrow alleyway through the wind and rain.

'How'd you get on,' she called, grabbing my arm to bring my head closer to her.

'Yeah, okay, quite interesting stuff,' I replied, as the scent of her perfume struggled with the smell of her damp coat.

'Lovely couple weren't they.'

I turned to see if she was saying this in jest, saw that she wasn't, and then cursed to myself, as the movement had flicked back my hoodie and rain was now going down the back of my neck.

As we neared the top of the road, I saw the slim figure of the woman from the first house coming out to the footpath. She had a long black raincoat on and a black shawl tied around her head. When she waved at me, I indicated to Diana she should get into the car.

'Who's that?' she asked.

'Not sure, no point in you getting wet,' I said, and walked over to join the lady in black at the letterbox.

'No mail at this time of night,' I called as I reached her.

She laughed and brushed back a strand of her long black hair as it escaped in a frizz from under the shawl.

'I just wanted to say I am sorry about Alistair before. He can get a bit testy,' she nodded slightly towards the house, where I could see the occupant pulling aside a lounge curtain to sneak a look at us. Up close, she did seem to be too young to be with such a grumpy old fellow but I thought 'it takes all sorts'.

'It's a bit wet for apologies. What's up?' I asked, immediately regretting the sharpness of the question as she looked a bit deflated, rather like a wet ball at the end of a winter game. But she got her puff back quite quickly and she stood closer to me so I could hear clearly.

'I've got something to tell you about the Brands but I can't tell you here, now.'

'Can I come in then?'

She shook her head.

'Is there somewhere we can meet tomorrow morning?' she asked, holding on to the side of my jacket to steady herself against the wind. 'Not in town? What about that café over at the beach?'

Perfect, I thought, I wanted to see Angelique there and then but tomorrow morning would be fine. We arranged to meet at 9 a.m., and she ran back inside as I crossed the road to the car.

'What was all that about?' Diana asked, as I tumbled into the passenger seat.

'She wants to have chat but not here, so we're meeting in the morning.'

'Oh, Bill's got a new girlfriend. I hope Angelique is okay with that?'

I just laughed and looked over at her. She had taken the time while I was talking for a quick tidy up. Her hair was perfectly formed once again, the coat tidied and straightened up.

'When you said the Brands were a lovely couple, you were joking weren't you?' I asked. We were driving down the hill from Brandsville and entering the back end of the town. The wind seemed to have fallen away.

'No, why? Everybody I talked to couldn't say too much about how they were loving and great neighbours. No problems apparently.'

'Are you sure about that?'

'Absolutely, why?'

'That's not the impression I got.'

'Who from – your new best friend?' Diana said, with what looked like a smirk, but I may have been mistaken.

'No, no, a couple of people I talked to.'

'God, you're hopeless. You've got it completely wrong.'

I looked out the passenger window as we approached the parking space where my car was sitting. In the rain and the wind, the only car on the street, it looked as lonely as I felt. Maybe I did get it wrong. But I had the interviews in my notebook. Maybe I had only heard what I wanted to hear.

'We'll meet with Harry in the morning and put our story together,' Diana said as we pulled up. Suddenly she seemed to be speaking from on high.

'Remember, I've got a meeting so let's talk afterwards.'

She nodded her head in the kind of affirmation people give when they don't really care. As she took off in the office car, I climbed into mine and sat for a minute pondering what had happened. I was cold now and gave a shiver, so started the car to help warm me up.

Harry was zoned out in front of the TV when I got home. Something to eat was in the microwave. It might once have been a stir fry and I must admit it didn't taste too bad once I heated it up.

During an ad break, Harry asked me how we got on. When I said we'd had mixed results, he said 'yeah, Diana told me', and held up his phone where I could make out a text, adding: 'We'll sort it out in the morning.'

I told him I had to meet somebody at Gordon's café first, which seemed superfluous since he probably knew already, then looked annoyed when I didn't even have her name. It did seem careless but when I told him where she and the old guy lived, he knew immediately who they were.

'That's Professor McGuigan. Alistair. Fell in love with one of his top students and ran off to the coast with her. Left his wife and kids. The whole lot, gone, silly old fool. Mind you...,' he said, bringing back the sound as the ads finished.

'How do you know him?' I said through a mouthful of rapidly cooling stir fry.

He gave me that look he does when you know immediately he'd be swearing and saying 'that's a dumb question' but he didn't say anything.

'Okay, just asking.'

'Now that you mention it, I did meet them at an art show a while ago,' Harry said.

'When did you go to an art show?'

'You know, it was that thing a few weeks ago when you went AWOL.'

I remembered it now. A big surf was holding up around the coast and, at short notice, I had to take off. As it turned out, I missed the best of it by a day but it was still good.

'Now shut up and let me watch my programme,' Harry said, turning the sound up as a way of putting a full point in the conversation.

21

ROS TAKES FLIGHT

The rain of the night before lingered in the morning. Harry had gone by the time I surfaced. A message from Diana on my phone said we needed to talk. I reminded her of my meeting at Gordon's, and ignored the reply. It wouldn't make any difference, so why bother. Harry called and, yeah, I had to go in. It was after 8 am but I reckoned on being okay for time.

Diana stood up and started walking over to Harry's office as soon as I came in. Pulling my note book out of my jacket pocket, I followed her in and sat beside her. The old man was looking out the window and turned when he heard us shuffling about.

'So Diana tells me the Brands were a perfectly normal, happy couple,' he said, addressing me. 'You got anything to add to this picture?'

'Maybe,' I said, but I hesitated.

'Maybe what?' Harry asked, and Diana turned to look directly at me.

'Some of the neighbours did hear some stuff going on before Brand died.'

'What sort of stuff?'

'Arguments, rows, cars coming and going, you know, that sort of thing.'

'So they had a few arguments,' said Harry, 'sounds like a normal couple.'

'Besides,' Diana added, 'everybody says they were a lovely couple and they're really shocked by the murder.'

'Who is everybody?' I said quietly.

'Everybody I talked to,' Diana said quickly, almost crowding out my sentence.

'Not everybody. For instance, the two directly next to the Brands on the side of the street where I was seemed to have heard and seen some goings on.'

'Oh those two old folks,' Diana said, waving a hand in the air. 'Isn't the old girl blind and the old guy pretty much deaf?'

'Not exactly reliable witnesses, Bill,' Harry added. 'Look, it all seems a bit flimsy so let's go with neighbours shocked by the murder and the Brands are a lovely couple.'

I looked at Diana. She seemed triumphant without having a grin, just that competitive look people have who want to win.

All I really wanted to do was to get out of there.

The wind had dropped and as I drove along the ridge above the beach I could see rain falling out to sea in random gangs rather than the massed movement of the night before. An annoying rain drop slid with a wriggle down the back of my neck as I walked up the path to Gordon's Café. She was already inside, hands wrapped around a cup. Early or late? Angelique came through the door from the back and, smiling, kissed me on both cheeks. I tingled with happiness, like when a kid gets slightly tickled, and returned the greeting in a clumsy bump of the heads. We laughed. I gestured to the table and ordered a coffee and a date scone. Angelique took the order and moved behind the counter, after a second glance.

'Hi sorry I'm late. Thanks for coming,' I said, taking off my jacket and sitting down.

'No, no, I'm a little early,' she said as she looked up from the book she was reading. Pulling back the frizzy black hair with her left hand she offered me her right.

'We didn't introduce ourselves last night. I'm Ros Peters, but I know who you are,' she said. Her hand was warm from the cup and her fingers long, slim and quite firm.

'Bill Brown.'

She knew this, she said, because the professor knew Harry, of course

'You prefer to go surfing than to take in high art apparently.'

'Oh, the art show but...' I was about to protest, but she smiled and told me not to worry.

Angelique came over with my coffee and scone, placing a light hand on my shoulder as she went past.

'Certainly a friendly place this isn't it? Or are you a special customer here?'

I wanted to answer her, to say I was in love, and had been in love with Angelique for a long time. She was my girlfriend, my partner or whatever. I just shrugged what was probably a sheepish smile.

'Yeah, something like that. So how is the prof? What's he up to now that he's retired?'

'Oh, he's not retired. He's just having a sabbatical.'

'Is that what it's called? I hear you're one of his students.'

She looked down momentarily and then with both hands pulled her hair back over both shoulders and looked at me directly.

'Alistair's burnt out. He needs a rest. He's writing his book.'

'Oh, what's it called? 'When Spring Meets Autumn'?'

I thought I'd pushed it a bit but she laughed then firmly corrected me.

'No, actually it's about what famous prisoners ate when they were incarcerated.'

'Okay, so how does that work?'

'Well, of course, where possible we have to experience it so he can write about the food.'

'So...'

'So at the moment we're having mealiepap for breakfast, like Nelson Mandela did when he was on Robben Island.'

'Sounds lovely. What's that all about? Like porridge?'

'Basically it's dried maize kernels ground down and served with milk and sugar. Although we don't have the sugar, of course, because it wouldn't be very authentic.'

'Of course,' I said, and muffled a laugh as I sipped the last of my coffee.

'Oh dear, would that be too much for you? I'm not looking forward to the next chapter. It's about what prisoners of war ate when in Changi prison.'

'Changi is...where, what?' I said, shaking my head.

'Singapore. It's where the Japanese tossed POWs during World War Two.'

'Yes, I knew that. So what's the food you are testing?'

'Rats.'

'That's gotta be fun.'

'Oh, in that case, I'll get Alistair to invite you and Harry to dinner then shall I?'

Leaning back, with my hands up, I declined the invitation. We were quiet for a minute and then she said she wanted to go for a walk on the beach. When I asked why, she didn't say anything but just stood and walked to the door. Waving to Anqelique, I followed. Roz was standing outside, pulling the collar up on her long black coat. She tied a black shawl over her hair, looking like she wandered out of the mist somewhere.

The rain wasn't at all heavy and the wind had gone right away, although I could feel it turning to the south as we crossed the road. She stood at the edge of the bank down to the beach. I jumped down and turned around to wait for her. Peering up, she seemed suddenly to soar in silhouette in the light rain, almost with a halo of light around her black hair, the long black coat and black boots. I thought she was going to float off and fly around the dunes, like a dark angel in the drizzle. In a way she did, because Angelique walked up behind her and Ros was flying through the air.

'Catch me,' she called, her arms out in front of her.

Before I could protest, she fell forward and I grabbed her waist. Her momentum pushed her body hard into mine, so my head was resting on her thin chest. The coat smelled of rain, and the frizz of her hair tickled my cheeks. I looked up and Angelique was looking down, her full lips suddenly pursed. She turned and walked back over the dunes to the café. I went to climb up and follow her but Ros grabbed my arm surprisingly strongly.

'It's okay, see her later. I need to talk to you now.'

We went down to below the high water line and walked along creasing wet sand below our feet. Spray from the sea stood high in the air around us. I was disturbed, but thoughts of Harry and Diana's insistence on another perception of the Brands drove me to ask Ros what it was that she wanted to tell me.

'It started a few months ago,' she said, her head down against the drizzle. The rain seemed heavier now we were out here on the beach. When I didn't prompt her, she glanced over at me and continued.

'I used to see Mariana Brand walking past our place. One day, I was out the front doing some gardening. Alistair's hopeless in the garden, so I try my best. Mariana is a great walker and has a terrific exercise regime. She's terribly fit.'

'That's one way of putting it, I suppose,' I said remembering the svelte figure at the funeral service, or did I just think it? Ros went on.

'We said 'hi' and this time she stopped and we had a chat. I was just starting up a book club and invited her to join. She wasn't too keen but we talked about books. It developed into a regular thing. Once a week, we'd have lunch, sometimes at my place or sometimes out. Never came over here, but we might in the future.'

Ros looked up at me and tucked a tangle of hair back under the hood of her rain coat. Her brown eyes sparked and she smiled.

'So you went out to lunch and...'

'Well, we never went to her place. I asked her once and she just said it was dreary and she wanted to get out. The property didn't look dreary to me. From the outside it seemed what might be called very now and shiny. I was happy enough with the arrangement as it's not my kind of place anyway.'

I was beginning to drift away. In the distance, further down the beach, I could just make out the figure of a fisherman at the water's edge.

'One day about a couple of weeks ago she didn't arrive to lunch so I rang her. Her voice was muffled and I could tell she was upset. So I went up there to her place even though she said she was fine. You know how it is when people sometimes say they're fine and you just know they're not. Alistair was against me getting involved but that's just him. He's so detached. I went up the road to her house. You have to activate an speaker system to gain entry through the gateway. I did and Ros answered, in what for her was a quiet voice. When I told her it was me, there was silence at first then the gate clicked and I walked in. Even before entering the house I thought it must be like living in a mausoleum.'

'Like in that Beirut song – *In the Mausoleum*?'

Ros looked at me again, so I spoke the words.

'Time travels to mourn
Your secret life
In your mausoleum'

'Yes, yes, something like that. Funny I'd thought of that too,' she said.

After walking up the wide white steps to the front door, Ros pulled the chain and bells sounded somewhere in the depths of the house. The sound they made was so impressive she thought there might even be monks swinging on the end of ropes. Nobody came to the door at first and she took a few steps back to try to see inside. Eventually the door was opened slightly and Mariana was standing in the doorway. She was beautiful, tall in a figure hugging dress down to the floor, and long sleeves covering her arms. Ros stepped in and went to hug her friend, noticing how she winced to her touch. Up close as she kissed her cheek she could see a bruise near her left eye. Mariana was normally impeccably dressed and well made up, so Ros sometimes thought it made them two unusual friends. This day, however, her make-up was heavier than usual but not sufficiently heavy to fully hide the bruise. Ros held her friend and looked up at the face before her. The eyes were distant. Just when she was going to ask what had happened, Mariana turned away and walked to the back of the house. Ros followed her into the kitchen. Mariana filled a coffee machine with water and Ros noted she had to use two hands to pick up the jug. As Mariana busied herself with the coffee things, Ros looked around the kitchen. It was modern in that glistening magazine home style. Vast in its own right. What struck Ros though was the view out the back. The window overlooked Coastlands and stretched down the coast to the distance. The backyard was pretty much covered in tiles, with some embedded shrubs and that long skinny grass that doesn't need cutting. A swimming pool was sunk into the ground on one side. Bush tumbled down the back of the hill over the boundary. It was idyllic in a southern California kind of way. Not my kind of thing, Ros said to me, but she could see the appeal. She felt Mariana come noiselessly alongside her and grasp her hand.

'Come, let us have coffee.'

They went into the open lounge. Ros remarked on how sunny it seemed on that autumn morning. They sat on the couch, Mariana still holding her hand. Ros wasn't too perturbed by the hand holding, although the grip was quite tight. She had become used to what she thought of as Mariana's Latin ways. She told Ros how she'd met Brand in Argentina, where he was on some council business. She'd been a model but had been under threat of having to go under the knife to keep up with younger models. Ros had expressed surprised and Mariana just laughed, but not happily, and said it was common. Mayor Brand had met her at a reception, where she and some of the girls from the agency had been paid to brighten up the scene. He pursued her, and she was enamoured with his macho ways, tales of the beauty of his country, his great standing in the community and life she might lead as the wife of an important leader of the community. So she came to marry Brand and live in a new country. At first she thought she loved him, and in a way she did. Being a Roman Catholic, she went to Mass and prayed to feel better about her marriage. She confessed what she thought was her sin to the priest, expecting to be condemned for her love of another woman, but he just told her all married couples went through periods of doubt. This was just one of those times. She thought this might be the case, but the more she prayed for her marriage the further she seemed to drift from Brand. Then, suddenly putting down her coffee cup, Mariana took both Ros's hands and pulled her close to her.

'I love somebody else. A person who I love so much but I can't have,' Mariana said pushing her face close to Ros's cheek.

Ros stopped in the sand. Even as the drizzly rain dripped down her face, her cheeks were red.

'I thought 'oh my gosh, I have a lover'. What am I going to do?'

Serious now, Ros told me this sort of thing hadn't happened to her for a long time but it did happen, particularly when she was younger. How young? I asked.

'Quite, quite young. Men and women seemed to want me to love them. I can't explain it but I felt bad about myself for a long time, like it was my fault.'

'Like Alistair?'

Ros shook her head. 'No, he is different,' she said, but I wondered how different.

I looked down the beach and could see the fisherman was Jimmy's dad. Mr Tatua was in the water using his surfcasting rod to cast the bait out beyond the waves to the fish.

Ros looked quite bedraggled now but she wanted to keep talking, and I didn't stop her. Mariana told Mayor Brand that she didn't love him anymore, omitting the minor detail that she probably never had, and she had met somebody else and wanted to leave him. They argued. Brand started in a low controlled voice but as Mariana's replies became more determined, he became more strident and louder.

'Who is he, this mystery lover of yours?' Brand said. She wouldn't say, too afraid of what he might do to Ros. He grabbed a handful of her sleekly shiny hair and pulled her close to him. 'Tell me or else,' he said, giving her a smack on the side of the face to reinforce his determination. He stood over her and was about to kick Mariana when she flung her hands up on outstretched arms and gave in.

'It's Ros, my friend Ros,' she said, a sob welling up in her throat. Brand dragged her up again by the hair demanding to know who Ros was and where she lived. He gave her a slap, hard, as a prompt. 'My friend Ros Peters. You know, I have told you many times how we have been meeting and talking about our love of books. I've fallen in love with her and cannot bear to be without her.'

'That curly-haired black bitch from down the road? The blown away hippy? You love her more than you love me?'

Mariana shielded herself as he raised his hand again. 'She doesn't know, she doesn't know, I haven't told her. Please don't do anything,' she pleaded, hanging on to his jacket to prevent him from leaving. 'You can hit me again but I don't love you and I don't know if I really ever did. Can't you forgive me for that?'

Brand suddenly seemed deflated, for a moment at least. Then he suggested that Mariana just had a crush on Ros and he was going away the next day, so they could both think about things and talk about it when got back. He reminded her of his status in the community and how he would be a laughing stock among the robust voters out there should it become known his wife had left him for another woman. They slept separately that night and Mariana stayed locked in her bedroom the next morning, not seeing off the mayor on his trip. She had met Stead at a function and called him the next day to talk about a complaint regarding Brand's assault on her. Instead of Stead alone, Brand's brother Gerry arrived as well. They talked it through into the early hours of the next morning. Gerry helped himself to his brother's extensive liquor cabinet, fell asleep and stayed the night. Stead left but came back several times to talk to Mariana, his reasoning wearing her down eventually to the point where it was decided she wouldn't press charges.

'They told her she was still beautiful and the bruise would quickly go away. Why ruin a career for a moment's passion? I tried to convince her to go ahead, clear the air and have him charged,' Ros said.

'But you wouldn't have wanted your relationship with Mariana to come out in court?' I said.

'I wasn't worried about that. I just wanted Brand and his mates taught a lesson. Besides, our relationship isn't like that; it can't be.'

The drizzle was clearing as we reached Mr Tatua. He was hauling in a fish and I waved at him.

'Hey Bill, come and give me a hand to land this,' he called.

I turned and Ros was walking away from me up the beach. 'Hey don't go,' I called. 'Is that it?'

'Yeah, pretty much I'd say. I do love Mariana and she is living with me and Alistair now, but only as a friend. That's why we didn't want you to come into the house last night. She doesn't want to talk right now,' Ros said, pre-empting my question, 'but I thought you should know.'

'Can I call you some time if I need to check something?' I asked, thinking that at the least Mariana might pick up the phone. Ros shrugged and turned away. Over her shoulder I could see the prof standing on the dunes waiting for her.

Mr Tatua had the fish in the shallows.

'Hey, let's at least have a look at this fish,' I called out to Ros. It was a bit flimsy but she did stop and turn. We walked down the beach to Mr Tatua. He'd just pulled in the fish and it looked like a good one. A snapper, it was not too big but I knew the old man would have full use of it all. He slipped the hook nearly from the fish's mouth and lay it down in the sea water as its swirled around his boots. The fish flipped and slipped away out through the incoming tide.

'They believe you should return the first fish you catch,' a voice said behind us. I turned, and it was Alistair. This morning he had tight jeans over his old rooster legs. A scarf wound around his neck.

'Oh, why is that Alistair?' asked Ros, stepping away from me and running her arm through his. She gave him a peck on the cheek. The drizzle kept on.

'It's bad luck to keep the first fish. It's a tradition.'

Mr Tatua was walking up through the water to where we were standing next to his fishing gear. Nice stuff it was too. Not cheap but well used. We greeted each other, and Alistair gave him a rather forceful hongi.

'Is that your first fish today?' I asked, probably a bit too loudly but the surf was taking breath so I had to raise my voice.

He didn't say anything but flipped open the lid of his bin to reveal three or four other fish, larger than the one he'd just thrown back. 'Nah, it just wasn't the one I wanted,' he said, smiling as he looked down at his catch.

Turned out he and Alistair knew each other already, as the prof was involved in helping in the preparation of a book about a project Mr Tatua and his community were part of, involving the building a waka. The boat was being built using traditional tools and materials, and Alistair's work was as a kind of archivist to record the process and eventually provide a documentary record once the waka was launched. The boat was completed, so they talked about the details of combining the official launch with the publication of the book. Alistair was a little behind in compiling the material, so Mr Tatua was giving him a deadline to work towards. One of the interesting things I picked up from the discussion was how the prof's progress had been interrupted by the drama around the Brands, the inclusion of Mariana in his nest with Ros and the mayor's tragic death. Mr Tatua knew all about this, which kind of surprised me but, in a way, it did make sense given the old man's connections and his son's work in the police.

Ros and I walked towards the dunes where Alistair had parked the car. The drizzle had eased up and the beach now looked grey from the sky right down to the damp sand. There was no wind and the surf behind us was formless, waves falling over themselves in a kind of aimless and powerless procession.

'What will you do with this now?' Ros asked, as we walked up to the car. 'This is just for your background, of course.'

'Not off the record as such?'

'No point really. Somebody will find out soon enough and I think it should be you.'

'Well, I won't quote you, if that's what you mean.'

Alistair was coming up the dunes towards us, so I thought it best to quickly wind things up and leave Ros. But before I could go, Ros held my arm and told me quietly to go and see Mariana while she diverted Alistair.

'Sorry, I have to go now but can I call you if I need any more help with this please?' I said loudly.

Ros, not looking at me but at the rapidly advancing Alistair, nodded. 'Text me,' I said quietly and, remembering I had a couple of worn cards in my jacket, quickly pulled one out and pressed it into her palm.

Angelique was serving when I walked back to the café but she saw me getting into my car and came out into the car park.

'What was all that about before?' I asked. 'Why'd you push her; you could've hurt her?'

Angelique actually smiled and tilted her head to one side, her eyes narrowing.

'Maybe. I just wanted to give her a message to stay away from you.'

'What? She is just trying to help me with this story.'

'You think so? You are a silly boy. I could tell by the way she looked at you and touched you that she wants you.'

Touched me? I didn't know that. I protested again, but was it a little too much?

'You don't know and you probably would never know,' Angelique said. 'She is probably tired of her old man and sees you as someone new and interesting.'

'I don't think so but you certainly gave me a fright. I thought she was going to take flight for a moment there and join the gulls over the bay.'

Angelique shrugged and kissed me on the cheek, turned and went back into Gordon's café.

22

MARIANA'S DROP OF WINE

Harry wasn't very impressed when I called and told him I wasn't coming into the office. He was quiet for a moment and I could imagine the office as a scene of elastic contentment. Not much noise, just people writing or reviewing. Christine smiling from over in the sports section. A poster of a sportsman in his shorts was pinned up next to a thoroughbred hitting the finishing post at speed. Diana looking up and down, sizing up the facts in front of her. Glen looking anxiously at the clock, probably checking Neil's story from the council meeting; one ear on the police radio.

'Where are you? We need to discuss how we're going to approach the story from last night,' Harry said.

'I thought that'd been decided, besides I've got bit of a problem.'

'Okay, but just give me the edited highlights.'

I quickly told Harry about how I had been told off the record that Brand knocked his wife about recently.

'On or off the record?'

'Background really, I guess.'

'A helluva a lot of use that is to us, Bill. You need to get here now so we can put this story together.'

I remained silent for a moment.

'Are you still there? When can we expect you? Either come in now or we're going with Diana's story.'

'Harry, I've just got to go and do something. Can you hold it?'

The last thing I heard was Harry using lots of swear words,

effing this and effing that.

Instead of turning into town I took the road to Brandsville. Climbing the road up this morning seemed like being elevated to a new world through clean washed bush. The rain had stopped and as I came out on to the plateau and turned to go into Brand Place the sun came through the morning sky. Down through the bush I could see the beach in the distance, where the heavy surf awaited an offshore wind to form up waves. I stood by the car for a moment, thinking 'tomorrow'.

Ros and the prof wouldn't be home for a while at least. I was confident of Ros's persuasive powers; that was my gamble anyway. I rang the bell but it was silent, so I softly knocked on the door so as to avoid alarming the occupant. Mariana Brand opened the door just as I was about to turn and go back to the office. It's true she had that beauty many men desire and many women crave. Almost as tall as me, with a long, angular face and deep brown eyes. But this morning the eyes looked nearly dead, as though they needed the kind of CPR only a night at The Strand could revive. I felt sorry for a moment about what I was going to attempt to put her through. So I started with the obvious.

'Hello, I'm William Brown from The Last Newspaper in the World. I'm sorry to bother you at this time but I really need your help.'

'Yes, how can I help you Bill? Why so formal now? Of course you met Ros this morning. I asked her to talk to you.'

'Oh, okay. Can we talk?'

She held up her phone, languidly giving it a wave in front of me, smiling slightly.

'See, it's okay. Ros has already sent me a message. She says maybe I can trust you. Can I trust you Bill?'

Can I trust myself? I thought, but looked straight at Mariana, and nodded the reassurance that, of course, she could. I think it must have been underwhelming, because she hesitated for a moment, then turned and walked through the hall without saying anything. I stepped through the open doorway and followed quickly. Pictures of old settlers hung on the walls down the hall. Doors led off to a bedroom on either side. The doors were closed so I couldn't see the bedding arrangements. We walked out into the lounge, which had more the look of transplanted academia. The prof must be right at home here. A long book shelf covered the back wall and files were piled a coffee table. A map of the district on a side wall was marked with arrows in red ink marking directions with black ink highlighting places of interests.

'The prof's been very busy,' I said as Mariana gestured for me to sit down on one of two arm chairs beside the heavily laden coffee table.

Instead of sitting, Mariana went over to a set of French doors and stood with her back to me, looking out at the contours of the backyard as it gently sloped in a mound down to the bush line. I couldn't see the beach from here but the Pacific Ocean would run in a line across the horizon had it not been obscured by a curtain of rain. Then again, I wasn't really looking at much except the curve of her back.

'Yes,' she said. 'Of course Alistair is busy. Why not? He is not very creative but Ros tells me he is most thorough.'

I wondered for a moment if she was talking about his writing.

'It must be quite difficult living here, you know what with...'

'What with the death of my husband or my relationship with Ros? Yes and no. It is most difficult with my home so close but it is not so difficult to be with Ros. Alistair, or the prof as you call him, has a greater understanding of natural society than most. He knows I love her.'

'That's pretty sanguine of him,' I said, borrowing a word I'd heard old Bernard use once. 'Sanguine?' Mariana asked.

'Cool?'

She nodded, and came to sit down on a sofa opposite me. She curled her legs up under her and looked like a wonderfully relaxed big cat waiting for its prey to come ever so closer.

A light from a piece of sun somewhere was shining from behind a hill around the side of the horizon. A thin coating of silver was painted under the clouds. The wind was going around, to offshore. The wind change distracted and may have made me impatient.

'Why did you kill your husband?' I asked.

'Why do you ask me?' Her mouth, a moment ago so light was now tight and her eyes chose to be closed.

'Because you did it, didn't you?'

Mariana stood, uncurling herself from the sofa and went over to bench between the lounge and the kitchen. She poured herself a glass of wine and tilted the bottle at me. I shook my head but she poured me one anyway. She was buying time but I was happy to wait, although maybe I should have hurried her along a bit. Her hand must have been shaking slightly, because some of the wine had spilt on to the tips of her fingers. The weird light outside reflected on to her skin, so her fingers seemed to have small stains of blood droplets. Mariana looked straight at me.

'Yes, I killed my husband.'

Now, I wasn't really expecting that reply. If I was, it was only a vague hope that a straight answer would spill. Of course, it was too easy.

'You looked surprised, Bill,' she said, and then reached over to touch the top of my writing hand. 'Do you really think I could shoot my husband?'

Again, she was too fast for me. She stood before I could reply and asked me if I wanted another drink even though I hadn't touched the glass. She was so tall standing in front of me.

'But you had motive. He struck you and threw you out,' I said, or rather mumbled. 'You also knew what he was up to,' I added.

'Up to?'

'Yes, we know about the sex, the drugs and the rock 'n roll.'

'I know it is early but you can help me dull the pain,' Mariana said as she turned and moved towards the bottle on the bench.

I downed my glass and held it up for a refill.

'You do feel pain don't you Mr Cool Surfer Dude?'

It was my turn to shrug.

'So why did you say you killed Mr Brand?' I asked. The wine was dry but I wasn't really paying attention. 'Murder isn't something you would want to admit to so casually.'

Mariana sat down opposite me and made a bowl with her hands around her glass.

'It is true that I didn't kill him but I feel like I murdered him,' she said, holding up the wine to the light in one hand and peering through the liquid. 'Do you understand what I am saying, Bill? Sometimes my English is not so good.'

I said I thought her English fine and maybe even better than mine. My phone was making noises, so I hauled it out and turned it off. It was my turn to stall.

'So you feel responsibility for his murder but you didn't actually pull the trigger?'

She looked down into the wine and swept it around the bowl of the glass.

'I may as well have. When I first met him, he was a dowdy provincial mayor with a lot of money. I believe I came to live here for love but maybe...' she drifted off for a moment. 'He was happy with the way he was but I wanted more.'

'More money?'

'I wish it was that simple. He had sufficient money but I wanted more.' A pause. 'Life –mi vida loca; my crazy life.'

'So you shot him?'

'With a gun?'

'That is usually the idea, yeah.'

Mariana was silent for an instant, looked down into the glass once more and then up to me.

'I don't need a gun to kill a man.'

'I'm sure Sergeant Stead would be interested in this interpretation of events.'

Her vibrant skin seemed to lose much of its lustre. She turned her head to one side. When I didn't say anything else, she again shrugged.

'Stead has been very caring to me. He's helped me very much since all this happened.'

'Okay, of course, Sergeant Stead is the most helpful man in Coastlands. Sorry, how do you kill a man, again, without a gun?'

'I may have placed my husband in the wrong place at the wrong time. He tried hard – too hard – to match what he thought were my aspirations for his life. He then became the man I did not know.'

'What about you? What did you become?'

She put the wine glass down and held up her hands palms up in exasperation.

'Yes it is true I became the woman he did not know but maybe I always was that woman he did not know.'

I could hear a car pulling up outside the house. Time was running out quickly. Now was the time.

'Mariana, please, what did you push Mr Brand into doing that may have got him a bullet in the head?' I asked, pointing a forefinger to my forehead.

I heard the front door opening. Ros was calling out 'hello' and Alistair was saying something about that reporter chap annoying Mariana.

'Please,' I mouthed to her.

'I made him what he was when he died. Corrupt and immoral and ready to take a risk he would never have considered without me. It was just too much for him.'

Ros and Alistair were now in the lounge. She was trying to shepherd him out into the kitchen but he was having none of that. However, Mariana stood and faced them both.

'It is good. Bill is going now and, so I will walk him out.'

Mariana seemed to take on power as she stood beside me. I could see how such power could attract and scare at the same time. Turning her head towards me, she nodded towards the doorway. I thanked Ros and Alistair for their hospitality. Alistair put up a hand.

'Before you go, when we met at the beach, I meant to invite you out to visit our project with Jimmy Tatua and his father. We are having a quiet prelaunch launch tonight.'

I said 'of course' but before I could say anything else, Mariana wrapped a hand around an arm and pulled at me to follow her up the hall.

'Do you understand what I am saying?' Mariana said as she leaned into me with her light frame as we walked to the door. She put her hand on the handle to open the door. I looked quickly over my shoulder down the hallway and then put my hand over her hand.

'So how did Stead help you then?' I said, turning face on to her.

'He was,' she looked down the hallway, 'very helpful in dealing with my poor husband afterwards.'

'Helpful how?'

'Are you okay Mariana?' I heard Alistair's voice from the end of the hallway.

'Of course,' she called back, and leaned over to me. 'You must ask Mr Stead yourself.'

That was something I planned to do straight away.

23

STEAD TO THE RESCUE

The Coastlands police station was one of the newest buildings in town. Rather than being a multi-storey concrete fortress like the old building, the new station was quite sophisticated. Three storeys high, it filled much of a block of land behind the main town centre. Built from some kind of new material, like a hard wood toothpaste, it was meant to be all eco-friendly. This new era approach seemed at odds with its purpose but it could be argued the cops were into recycling in a big way. We'd all had a tour when it first opened recently; lots of glass, very open. Also lots of cameras but that was to be expected. The occasional buzzer but otherwise very quiet or maybe just well soundproofed. Harry had muttered about there probably being the same old clients. His suspicion seemed confirmed a couple of nights later. Listening to the police scanner, we heard an officer describing a suspect he was looking for as 'wearing a tangerine baseball cap, on backwards'.

I had called ahead, so Stead quickly came down to reception when I arrived.

'Are you here to help us solve this murder?' he asked, without any movement in his face.

I waved him to lean forward, and put my mouth closer to his ear.

'No, I think you mean suicide don't you Mr Stead?'

He turned his head around straight away so his face was right in mine.

'You had better come through.'

A buzzer went and the door swung open.

'Do you want an interview room?' the duty officer called from the desk.

'No, no it's not that kind of visit,' Stead said, waving me towards the stairs, saying to me 'Let's go to my office.'

It was true the new police station was an improvement on the old one. That building looked like somebody had dropped a giant block of concrete on the ground and proceeded to fashion a police station from a template. I did wonder whether there was still the mythical basement where difficult prisoners were processed. Stead flashed his card as we went through humming glass doors. Offices were visible on each side as the wooden beams curved up to the ceiling. From where we walked I couldn't see them, but I knew, the cells below were actually reinforced glass boxes enabling the officers on duty to have a clear sight of all the cells. I was struck how a building of enforcement could also be a thing of beauty.

Stead buzzed us into his office, its walls of exposed timber giving off a golden glow even in the winter.

'Nice office,' I commented as Stead sat behind a practically paperless desk.

'Head office reckons we'll be more productive if we see more light,' he said, then shook his head. 'So what's all this suicide rubbish you're talking?'

'It's not rubbish, it's a story, and a good one,' I said. I raised my hands up as though scoping a large headline, adding: 'How about 'mayor's suicide cover up' or 'top cop in the gun over mayor's death'?'

'Too long,' Stead said, and sat back in his chair.

'What?'

'The last one, you know 'top cop in the gun', it's too long. I don't think your old man would go for it.

'Because it's got too many words?'

'Nah, because it isn't going to happen is it?'

It was my turn to sit back in my seat, and then I got my phone out.

'Look, I want to record this interview.'

'Who said anything about an interview, put that thing away,' Stead said firmly, leaning forward now.

'Why? Why should I?'

'Well, for one thing, you won't want this on the record and neither will Harry.'

That surprised me and I wondered why Harry wouldn't want me to keep a record. I shrugged and thought how I could get around this situation, but before I could say anything, Stead stood up and came around from his side of the desk to sit in a chair next to me. He really did enjoy invading my space, I thought.

'You're a really clever guy when you try and in this case it looks like you've tried too hard,' he said.

'Is that meant to be a compliment or an admission?'

'Neither. Let's put it like this – why do you think Harry sent you to cover the story in the first place?'

'Because he knew I was bored and thought it'd be good for me to do something useful?'

'Yes, I suppose 'useful' is the right word.'

'You don't mean useful in the way I mean useful do you?' I said, trying to not look embarrassed by my perceived uselessness.

'That's the boy, you're catching on. Why did you think I showed you Mr Brand's body like that?'

'It did seem a bit odd, but you said you owed Harry and we both know what that was about.'

It was Stead's turn to look uncomfortable, but I noticed that it was only a mild discomfort.

'So you framed the mayor for his own murder.'

'That's a bit twisted even for you,' he said, the rock wall that was his face cracking a slight smile.

'Okay, so Mr Brand ended up in a ditch with a hole in the front of his head, with you standing next to him, and Harry's given, sorry, a head's up.'

'That's what it looks like, yeah. Well, you were pretty convinced and so was everybody else.'

'So who put him there? Was it you?'

'Does it really matter?'

'I'd say so wouldn't you?'

'Let's just say he arrived where he was at his own hand.'

'So there was that final call to Mariana and then 'bang' it's all over?'

'Maybe, something like that,' Stead said, his voice trailing away before I urged him to tell all.

The way Stead told it, Mayor Brand's brother Gerry had called Stead at home. He could hear Mariana sobbing in the background as Gerry outlined the situation, so he drove quickly around to the house from where he lived in Brandsville. Mariana seemed more composed than Gerry when Stead arrived at the house. She told him how she had received a call from Brand saying how he loved her and couldn't bear the shame of losing her. He admitted things had gotten the better of him, the business was a mess and he was forced to do things he hated. Mariana had looked up from her seat in the pristine lounge and commented 'Well, he still did bad things.' Stead told her to go on. Brand told Mariana to call Gerry, and that she would be well taken care of in the future. He said he was at Drain Road in Waterslea. Mariana asked why he was there and told him he should come home. Brand said this was where his grandmother lived and where he had always felt safe, which Mariana always thought was strange because Brand had always referred to the area as a 'damp hole'. Mariana heard a single shot.

Stead told Gerry to stay with Mariana, and drove down to Drain Road. He drove slowly, making sure not to draw attention to his car in any way. Waterslea was about 10 minutes away from Brandsville but Stead said it felt like the drive took an hour. He drove slowly along Drain Road peering through the winter night until he came up to the mayoral car. Finding the car empty he used his hand torch, keeping the light as low as possible, to find Brand slumped backwards with his head under water in the drain. Stead was in a quandary, because if he went closer he would leave footprints around the drain and the body. He went back to his car and found the night vision binoculars he used on stake outs and searches. Crouching low, he could see more details of Brand's body with his head under the water. Stead let out a breath before carefully retracing his steps along the road to his car where he put on a pair of gumboots. He made his way carefully down the bank and walked along beside the drain. He'd seen a lot of bad scenes but even Stead felt something awful as he approached the body. He found the gun, a neat little revolver and carefully picked it up off the ground. He couldn't see Brand's cell phone straight away but saw it out the corner of his eye reflecting the shallow torchlight more than an arm's length away from the body, partially submerged on the edge of the water.

He drove back to Brandsville, this time at what seemed a faster pace than before. He broke the news to Mariana and Gerry. Brand's brother swore, then burst into tears; his wife, just nodded and sat silently. He was able to formulate something resembling a plan as he had driven back from Waterslea. Gerry would stay at the house with Mariana, saying she had called him concerned by the circumstances of Brand's departure. Stead would go home for a few hours before going in early, but not too early, to his office at the police station. He would chat to the duty officer, then go to his office to be ready when Mariana called to tell him at 5 am to say her husband hadn't returned home after unexpectedly being called away to a meeting at Waterslea.

'You slept?' I asked.

"How do you mean?"

"When you went home."

'Of course, why not?' Stead asked in reply.

'Nothing. So you woke up on time then?'

'What do you think?'

Stead was in his office at 5 a.m. when Mariana put her call into him. He gave the duty officer a message to say he was going out to Waterslea to look. This was something of a risk as ordinarily he came and went relatively freely, but it was a risk he was prepared to take. He drove out to Drain Road but he could see the figure of farmer Elliott Hale standing next to Brand's body as he approached the drain. Hale looked to have just arrived as he was still on his farm quad-bike, his back to the road as he stood up to peer at the body in the drain. Stead slowed down and thought quickly, he could quietly cruise on down the road and leave the farmer to report the death. He pulled up on the road next to the drain and sounded his horn. Hale turned and waved him over urgently. Stead climbed out of his car, put his boots on and met the farmer down by the drain.

'Thank God you are here,' Hale said, 'looks like you've turned up at just the right time Mr Stead. That's our mayor right there; he's pretty dead. Did somebody call you?'

'Yeah, his wife. She was very worried. He was to come out here for a meeting but didn't come home. And now here he is.'

'Strange place for a meeting,' Hale said as he crouched down. Stead was worried the farmer would notice the extra set of boot prints, so he quickly walked down over the ground to check the mayor. After looking down at the mayor's body, he turned and looked up at Hale.

'Well, you know these tycoon types; they're always popping up for meetings all over the place.'

'He won't be popping up anywhere soon, poor sod,' Hale said, with a farmer's practicality.

'Yeah, look, don't worry about it. I'll call this in and tell them you found Mr Brand. I can take your statement while we wait, so you won't have to worry about this anymore.'

'Sweet,' said Hale, as practicality ruled.

So it was done.

'So you guys rallied around to help, that's okay, but why would you do that?'

'You know there's a group of us who really want to see this

place turned into something special. We want Coastlands to reach its full potential and Mr Brand was our leader in that cause.'

'But things went places he wasn't quite prepared to go to?'

'I guess you could say that. No, he went there alright but there's a difference in inheriting a property development company and doing the job yourself. His old man was much more ruthless.'

'What about Mariana? She is devastated and believes she caused him to commit suicide after all?'

'Yes, that's true but she had a couple of million reasons to go for our option.'

'Life insurance. The company wouldn't pay out on a suicide?'

'It's a classic win, win.'

'Except for the mayor I suppose. In the meantime, the search for the murderer will go on. Then what? It's not going to look good on your career record.'

'What is it that Harry likes saying 'Coastlands Cops – they never get their man'?' Stead said. 'Besides, I love this place, why would I want to get promotion and have to leave?'

'Harry's going to love this isn't he?'

'I don't think so, buddy, he's as involved as the rest of us.'

'Apart from the blood on your hands.'

'Well, there is that I suppose. But, yeah, you go and talk to your old man and see what he says. You'll probably find he won't have a bar of your daft theory that the mayor killed himself.'

Stead stood up. I remained sitting for a moment but he jerked his head towards the door. As we walked down the stairs, Fish Marren came up the other way. He and Stead stopped and had a talk while I continued on down. Stead caught up with me at the bottom of the stairs.

'We're going to have a briefing on how the murder inquiry is going.'

'So Fish...'

'What do you think? Say hi to Harry,' Stead said as he opened the door to let me out.

24

DEATH BY LIFE

So Brand wasn't evil. He was just another politician who over-extended his credit in the reality bank. At some point, he must have woken up one morning and realised that his fantasy world had slid irreversibly into overdraft. This was the simple explanation of what Mariana meant but it did confirm what I thought: that Brand had been thrust into a position of power and greed. One or the other, or probably even both, did for him in the end. I had guessed Brand was involved in something and was out of his depth. I wondered if he had seen an albatross, foreshadowing his downfall: maybe it was the whole mix of the developments involving overseas investors, the land, and the downtown precinct of our coastal town.

As I drove down the hill into town, I could see a good surf was starting to build up at the river mouth bar. Still a bit heavy, but a few guys were already paddling out. I parked the car and walked up the road to the office. Neil was coming the other way, from the direction of the council office. He didn't see me at first, as he had his eyes down on his phone. We nodded at each other and I led him up the stairs to the office. Near the top, I stopped and he almost fell over. I turned and held his arm.

'Sorry,' I said.

'No, no,' he said, holding up his phone, 'my fault, but why did you have to pull up just then?'

'It just occurred to me I had to be somewhere else.'

'Had to be or wanted to be?' Neil asked. I turned aside so he could pass. I was about to go down the stairs when he added: 'You really should make you your mind what you want to do and stop wasting the old man's time.'

His words made me hesitate. I stopped one step down, turned and looked at him. I usually ranged over Neil but this time, from the top of the stairs, he comfortably looked down on me, standing his ground as if to make a point. He was a nice guy. I reached out a hand as if to reassure him. Neil reacted as if I was going to give him the Coastlands handshake and took a step back. He turned and went through the office door. I followed and went over to chuck my jacket down by the desk.

Diana looked at me as I sat down and started flipping through my notebook. She looked back at her screen. I thought how she and I were in some ways alike, but she was better at it. It was like where physiotherapists use mirrors to convince patients the bad pain in their limbs has gone away by showing a reflection of the good limb. When I looked at Diana maybe I saw the good journalist I could be – professional, interested, enthusiastic, studious and energetic. Her image reflected back to me and helped me to forget the pain and believe I was a better, more competent person. This wasn't love but more like a reflected admiration. I wasn't sure Angelique would understand and I didn't want to see Diana tumbling down the stairs.

Harry was staring intently into his screen and continued to as I stood at his doorway. Glen came over to me.

'He's not happy,' Glen said quietly.

I thought he looked serious. His fingers tapped the desk, then his keyboard, then his desk.

'You'd better get your story straight. Any story will be better than usual.'

'What 'usual'?' I asked.

'You know, a good surf was running, that sort of thing.'

'As it happens the surf was shit but it is pretty nice now, so maybe I'll head off.'

'Don't be an arsehole Bill,' Glen said. I was a bit surprised as it was unlike him to talk to me like that but probably understandable in the circumstances.

Out of the corner of my eye I saw Harry look up at us, then stand up. He ignored me and quietly asked Glen to pull in Diana and Neil in for a meeting. He didn't look at me or mention me by name. As Glen turned to leave I held his shirt sleeve in a not very committed manner.

'Glen, it's okay. I think I've got the story.'

He pulled out of my grasp with a shake of his head and went over to talk to Diana and Neil. I went back to my desk but didn't sit down. A coffee seemed a good idea so I went into the cupboard we called our tea room. Christine was there, mixing herself a drink. She smiled and we chatted. I remembered her story about the mad night at the Mount. Looking into her eyes I wondered how come she was so nice. I put down my cup and suggested she join us, then turned to walk over to Harry's office.

All the chairs were taken, so Christine and I stood. Harry was about to say something to me but I put up my hand to stop him. His mouth opened then shut.

'Don't tell me what to do,' he said. 'Where've you been? In this job, I call and you answer? And don't try to shut me up. I might be your grandfather but here I am also your boss. Glen, tell him.' I looked around at Glen who sort of grimaced and smiled at the same time.

'Well, Bill, it's like this,' Glen started but stopped.

'Mayor Brand committed suicide,' I said and was surprised by the silence as I looked around the team to Harry. 'And before you say any more, I want an apology from you.'

Harry looked at me with his mouth open. Glen couldn't quite stop his eyes from flicking open and shut in quick succession. I could hear Diana's quiet laugh but I noticed Neil's lights go on.

'Where the hell did you get that from?' Harry said. 'Did you dream that up sitting on your bum at the beach?'

I wasn't worried by Harry's response. It was expected under the circumstances.

'Speaking of bums, do you mind if I grab a seat,' I left and wheeled in a couple of office chairs for Christine and me. As I did so, I felt something I hadn't before. It was a determination to tell the truth as I saw it rather than as it was being told by others. It didn't necessarily occur to me then that it was the same determination I felt when paddling through a heavy surf to get out the back and into some waves.

Harry sat back in his chair, interested, I thought. I pushed the chair around beside Neil, so I was on the right hand side of Harry's desk, with nobody between us. 'Speak to me,' Harry said. Diana leaned forward, and I looked at Neil who nodded at me.

'We know some nasty stuff has been going on around the place but it's been very hard to pin down, right?'

'Defamation laws,' said Harry.

'Yeah, defamation laws,' Glen repeated.

'Neil has found the mayor's involvement in some interesting deals involving property. Some of his bedfellows are, well, bedfellows, so...'

'But you can't write that,' said Neil.

'Defamation laws,' I said.

'Yes, defamation laws,' he said.

'Yes. Even so, the mayor was apparently very successful. He was at the forefront of bringing new business into the town when this place really needed to go forward.'

'Right,' said Harry in that kind of drawn out way indicating uncertainty but interest, which was encouraging.

'Just before his death, Brand split with his wife,' I said, then held up my hand. 'No, sorry it was the other way around. He smacked her one and she chucked him out.'

'What? Why?' Harry said.

'Did she find out what he was up to?' Diana asked.

'Sort of, yes, but it was the other way around. In his own clumsy, small town way he was trying to meet her high expectations.'

'High expectations? He was just the mayor of a coastal community,' she said, rather harshly I thought. Maybe Harry thought so too, because he looked under his eyelids towards her for a moment.

'That's probably not the way he sold her on the idea of marrying him and coming here to live is it.' Neill said.

'Well, as I understand it, she was under the impression he was some kind of wealthy political king-pin on the rise.'

'Well, he was, kind of but in a very small pond,' Diana said.

'Yes, but she had very high expectations and he started getting into some interesting stuff. They became more and more distant and she started to become increasingly attached to her friend.'

'Who?' said Harry. When I didn't say anything, he raised his eyebrows and held his hands apart like he was preparing to catch a ball.

'Ros,' I said, and thought 'how did he do that, he's good'.

'What? Not the...'

'Your mate the prof's girlfriend. That's where she is now, staying with them.'

'This gets better. A threesome with old Alistair. That has to be bullshit,' Harry said. 'How do you know?'

'No, no, no, it's not a threesome or anything. They're just good people looking after her.'

'Like I said, how do you know? Even you can't make this sort of shit up.'

I was a bit put off by that comment but continued.

'I've spent the morning talking to Ros and Mariana.'

'How'd you get past Alistair? I'm surprised he let you anywhere near them.'

'He's okay. No I met Ros at the beach and we talked. She told me everything.'

'How was the surf?' Neil said quietly.

'Shit, but hey that's fine, because this is more important.'

'And?' Harry said, leaning forward. I think he was interested.

'Then Alistair arrived. I left them to it and went and had a nice chat with Mariana.'

'A nice chat. Where?'

'At Alistair's place.'

'This just gets better. Did he say you could go there?'

'No, I just went.'

I saw Glen smile slightly and nod his head. Then I told them how Mariana blamed herself for Brand's death.

'Bullshit,' said Diana vehemently, to which I agreed.

'But what about Sergeant Stead and all that stuff with the cops if it was simply a suicide,' Glen asked.

'Yes, that's interesting isn't it? We know that Stead and his mates have been up to some nasty stuff. That he's a mate of the mayor and his brother. So maybe they were protecting the family.'

'And their financial interests?' Neil put in. I noticed he was holding his phone below the table.

'What I don't get,' Glen said, 'Is how come you got involved in this story in the first place?'

'How do you mean?' Harry said quickly.

'Well, let's face it. Your grandson is a bit of a deadbeat around the office, sorry Bill,' Glen said.

'No offence taken,' I said. 'Yeah why did you send me out to the scene, Harry? After all, it's not every day we have a murder in Coastlands. I'd have thought Diana would be first pick, she is the best out there.'

Diana's head jerked back and she went to open her mouth, but Harry put a hand up to stop her.

'What can I say? You surprised me, coming back with that pic of the dead mayor. Stead was meant to just show you how it was a murder. You'd come back, write up your story and go for a surf. Job done. But you had to go off on one of your tangents.'

The room was quiet. Harry swivelled his chair to look at the window, like it was his turn to be lost in the horizon.

'So it was a cover up?' I asked.

'And you were involved, Harry,' Glen said.

'Hmm, not exactly but I knew something was up when Stead specifically asked me to send you out to the scene. He said if I sent you, we'd get a good result. It seemed worthwhile at the time. I should have known, after all he wasn't your number one fan. I guess a part of me just wanted to challenge you, to see you get interested in something. I thought this might hook you. I was right wasn't I?'

Beside me Neil continued to look down at his phone. Next to him, Diana crossed her legs and opened her mouth, then closed it again. Neil cupped a hand around his chin and looked intently at Harry.

'I don't know old man,' Glen said. 'Why go to all that trouble to cover up his suicide. Tragic as it was, surely it wouldn't be the end of the world for Coastlands.'

'Not for Coastlands but for the Brand family and the mayor's crew maybe,' Neil said, looking up.

'How so?' Glen asked.

'One of the things I've noticed is that it's been terrifically hard to access records of any kind at the council since all this went down. It used to be pretty open right up until recently, and now nothing. So something was definitely up, I think.'

'And not just in a business sense,' Diana said. 'I'm betting they didn't want that business with Mrs Brand coming out either. By the way, Harry, will she get an insurance pay out on the murder?'

'So I understand,' Harry replied, shifting in his seat, 'but that's normal.'

'Not on a suicide though,' Diana said.

'No,' Harry and Glen said at the same time. Harry looked over at Glen and gave a shrug.

'Suicide as failure,' Neil said quietly.

'What?' asked Harry.

'It's the Graham Greene theory: suicide is sort of the ultimate failure.'

'Where'd you get that from?'

Neil held up his phone, adding 'It's quite interesting really. The quote is from *The Other Man, Conversations with Graham Greene* by Marie-Francoise Allain.'

'Yes, very interesting but I think you will find he believed that failure was a 'sort of death',' Harry said.

'A death by life then?' Neil replied.

'So what are we going to do with my story,' I asked nobody but in reality I was addressing Harry. He didn't say anything.

'Nothing much I guess,' said Glen, then looked at Harry and added: 'We can't expose the cover up without compromising ourselves can we?'

Harry didn't say anything but gave a shrug and turned away from us. We sat in silence for a moment, and then Glen got up and left the room. The others followed him out but I remained sitting with Harry. We didn't need to talk anymore.

25

ON BEING HERE

It was winter dark by the time we had finished. Instead of going home, or joining the others at The Strand, I drove over to the beach. The air was much cooler now but the wind had dropped and there was no rain. A half-moon provided a dim light. The store and café were closed with only night lights on. Grabbing a jacket from the back of the car, I walked over the dunes to the beach. Foam glittered in the moonlight on rows of even waves. Suddenly I felt very calm but sad that my home town was changing forever. I turned to look back and saw Angelique standing on top of the dunes behind me wrapped in a blanket. I walked up to her through the sand, feeling like I was wading through quicksand. When I reached her, she said nothing but opened the blanket to fold me into her. We stood together. It was warm.

A light flickered somewhere and turning around we could see a 4 x 4 coming down the hill with its warning lights on.

'What's that do you think?' I said.

'I don't know,' she said. 'Let's go and have a look?'

Reluctant as I was to leave behind the moment, I followed Angelique down to the road. As the vehicle came down the hill and drew closer to the T junction by the store, I saw that it was a police vehicle driven by Jimmy. It was towing a large sea-going waka his people had been building. We had featured a story on it recently, something to do with carvings. The boat was being built to commemorate the past and connect the tribe. Jimmy nodded to me as we walked over to the truck when it stopped at the junction.

'Jimmy, hi. Does Mr Stead know you've borrowed this truck?' I asked.

'Of course, it was his idea.'

His father sat beside him, with Mariana, Ros and Alistair in the back and the crew in a convoy of vehicles behind them. They drove over to the beach access and backed the trailer down on to the sand until they reached the hard, wet sand. Angelique and I went back up on to the dunes to watch. The crew had parked their vehicles and walked down with their gear to the beach. When they were ready an old woman said a prayer and Mr Tatua led a haka. He said something to Jimmy, who stepped away from the others and waved to us. We went down the beach, the blanket licking the light sea breeze. Ros and Mariana stood to one side with Alistair.

'The old man has invited you on board,' Jimmy said, nodding towards his father who was making final preparations for the launch.

I felt the palm of Angelique's hand on my back, saying farewell as I quietly stepped forward. We were in a good area for a launch. The swell was a little lower as the current ran out from shore. Jimmy backed the trailer into the shallows and we heaved the waka seawards. Mr Tatua signalled me to climb on board next to him at the rear. Jimmy took up the steering oar behind us and the crew began to paddle hard through the lines and out beyond the surf. I looked up and the sky was clear now, the moon lighting the bay like it was extra day. Standing unsteadily next to Mr Tatua, I looked back to the beach and saw Angelique fully encased in the blanket. I didn't know where we were going, but I knew where I was.

ABOUT THE AUTHOR

Mick Stone is the pen name of Michael R. (Mike) Smith, who lives
in Rotorua, New Zealand, where he is an independent writer,
editor and publisher.

MORE BMS BOOKS

Enjoyed this book? The following list of books is available from BMS Books.

A Soldier's Life by Lou Geraets

My Life...the Meanderings of Pop Knill by Lou Geraets

The Forgotten by Sarah Groot

Forestry, People and Places – Selected Writings from Five Decades by Dennis Richardson

Demons Inside My Mind – Life with Anorexia – Jenna Oldham

For more information, contact:
BMS Books
5 High Street, Glenholme
Rotorua 3010
New Zealand
Email: ms@bms.co.nz
URL: www.bms.co.nz
Tel: 64-7-349 4107